nothingland

other books by katherine silva

<u>The Wild Oblivion</u>
The Wild Dark
The Wild Fall
Hallowed Oblivion
Lost Oblivion
Orchards
Dan & Andy's Scary-Oke Holiday

<u>Deadlands</u>
Undead Folk
Dead Folk
Nothingland

<u>The Monstrum Chronicles</u>
Vox: Book 1
Aequitas: Book 2
Memento Mori: Book 3
Acquolina: A Short Story

The Collection
Night Time, Dotted Line

nothingland

book 3
in the deadlands

by
katherine silva

Published by Strange Wilds Press
Print first edition: December 20th, 2024
E-book first edition: December 20th, 2024

Cover design by Katherine Silva
www.katherinesilvaauthor.com
Strange Wilds Press Logo by MartaLeo
Cover photos courtesy of Pexels and Unsplash

ONE

Black and white flashed as the tunnel narrowed... Death arrived for everyone eventually. Janet found herself wondering which of the two colors she should move toward when her time came.

Sunset radiated over the horizon as the train cleared the mountain passage, as the whistle blew solemnly. Janet turned her attention to the open cargo car door before her and the emptiness of the rail yard as it rumbled by. Dozens of tracks meandered and criss-crossed one another in a dizzying display across the ballast. Disused cargo cars in muted rust colors sat like forgotten blocks.

The train slowed. Janet summoned everything she had to get to her feet. Her legs wobbled and she caught sight of the rash surrounding her latest tattoo: words from her beloved father, Amos, written in dedication to his husband, her dad, Hugh.

"You need to stay focused." The memory of Hugh's voice enshrouded her with warmth despite of the frozen early morning temperatures. When she was a child, he always knew how to keep her focused when the world spun too fast.

"I know you're tired, but you can't fall down here. You have to find the Junco."

The map Hugh had left her on the penthouse floor of the Hierophant Hotel was as plain as it was puzzling. It pointed to where she would find her quarry: Steele, the man who had taken everything from her. He'd had Amos killed which made Hugh do the only thing he thought he could do to protect her…become one of Steele's hit men.

Steele had taken any normal life she could have had and twisted it away. Who knew how many other people he'd done this to over the years.

He needed to be stopped and she was going to stop him.

The train crawled along the track. Janet braced herself to jump down but the slow steady sway of her legs as she fought for balance made her wary of going too soon. Normally, she'd have hopped already. She'd be half way across the yard by now making her way toward the glow of sunlight on the horizon. But everything was on fire in her body and in her mind. She'd scratched that tattoo into herself days ago with an old pen, a lighter, and mania driving her on. Her body saw fit to rebel now.

The train shuddered to a stop. Not expecting the sudden jerk of the car, Janet crumpled from the opening down into the rocks. Her knees and palms screamed as they took the brunt of the impact.

"*Get up, Ella,*" Hugh urged her.

She struggled to her feet, then pushed her heels and toes through the ballast to crossed the yard. Further and further away from the train, she found herself amongst dirt hills and scrub. Plants shifted in the light breeze. The only sound was the steady whoosh of wind in her ears it fought to carry her away on its gusts and the hood of her jacket flapping against her back.

It was hard to tell from the map how far the train yard was from Nothingland, the sprawl circled in giant red pen at the center of Hugh's map. It could have been a couple miles. It could have been twenty.

As she cleared the first hill, she stumbled on a large rock and went down onto her hands and knees again. This time, her stomach came unglued with the violent drop. She imagined it hula-hooping around her middle as she vomited. All that came up was bile and saliva.

"I know it hurts, darling. But you're going to survive this," Hugh whispered. She imagined him cupping her soft, child-like hand in his own when she was a girl: when she'd stuck her finger on a thorn, or picked up a pretty piece of broken glass in the train tunnel, when she cried at night because she was so, so hungry… How many times had he said that to her?

"Focus, Ella."

At her back, she felt it: the shadow. A cold prickling ebbed against her skin as she swung her head up, hair sticking to her sweat-laden face. Lights glimmered in the valley down below, hanging bulbs strung around temporary wooden poles. Someone was down there. Judging by the number of metal trailers and tents, lots of someones.

On her feet once more, Janet shambled down the hill toward the trailers. At the bottom, she suddenly had the thought: what if they were dangerous? What if they saw her and immediately saw a defenseless, fucked-up woman? The dread nearly pinned her in place. Her hand scooped the wrench from her tool belt, dried with the blood and brain matter of Steele's lieutenants back at the Hierophant Hotel.

They'd just have to be surprised when she didn't go down without a fight.

The canvas tents whipped in the wind as she got closer, as she took in the pale red lights creating a hanging border for the strange little camp. A sound reached out to her that she couldn't quite identify: like someone dropping nails on a metal floor. Once she peered around the corner, her eyes widened in sudden recognition.

A cage on wheels was hooked to one of the trailers, its metal siding below the bars decorated in bold colors with flourished letters. Centurion's Magical Carnival. Janet immediately dropped into a memory from her childhood of the circus rolling into town and turning the nearby park into a glorious labyrinth of striped tents, bright lights, and wild animals.

The creature pacing back and forth in the cage stopped to regard her, shining eyes flickering like pennies. Its sheer size kept her frozen in place, the muscles like liquid gold beneath its smooth fur, bones faintly showing around its ribs. A lioness. She'd seen one as a child at the Centurion's fair that popped up in Town. It probably wasn't the same one. Couldn't be after close to ten years but, then again, maybe it was?

Hypnotized by its stare, Janet wondered faintly if she could go anywhere and not have it stalk her silently from its enclosure. The longing in its eyes her told her it was hungry. She could tell it was assessing her as either a potential meal or threat. And she hated the impulse that throbbed in her to unlock it from its cage. How long had that poor, poor animal been trapped like this? Forced to perform and entertain in order to survive? It wasn't right.

But now wasn't the time to let a voracious animal out even if she could find the keys. She needed to find a place to lay low until she could rest. She needed to—

The animal chuffed at her, the sound echoing in through the small space as its head bobbed up and down.

The scuffs of boots alerted Janet moments before she wrestled herself behind the other side of a tent. A metal door banged against the outside of the trailer towing the cage and footsteps crunched in the dirt.

"Easy, old girl," someone muttered. "What are you making noise for?"

The voice made Janet want to abandon her hiding spot. If not for her staunch paranoia, she might have. While it wasn't familiar to her, the timbre was laced with concern for the beast and that filled her with a kind of hope she hadn't had in what felt like forever. A hope she hadn't felt since she had watched her fox friend playing in the grass behind her old home.

Before he was killed.

Before she found out *who* killed him.

Her momentary lick of anger was snuffed out by a darkness falling across her along with the pinch of sorrow.

Janet toppled over like a teetering tower. Her eyes wouldn't open; gravity pinned her to the dirt. A few sprigs of grass tickled her sweltering forehead and cheeks. Whatever lingering pieces of Janet's brain that were still coherent gradually began to sink in the mire of exhaustion.

Fingers touched her shoulder. "Who are you then?" Her wrist. "Fuck. You're not doing so—"

Their voice was muffled as Janet lost herself in a memory from long ago, tinged by amber lights and fledgling horror. A time when she still had her fathers there to protect her from the shadows in the night.

TWO

Ethereal terror slipped like poisonous fumes through young Ella as she slept, the kind of vapor that left no trace, no smell, no visible wisps curling in the air, the kind of fear she didn't even know was coiling her up until the screech happened. It tore her from the feathers of her dreams, the sound battering around in her brain as she tried to grasp it, as she tried to understand exactly what it is… What was this thing that had burrowed in and scratched her out of a calm sleep?

It mounted up again, so loud this time that it sent her heart bounding and skipping. Ella screamed. How did it sound so far away and so close at the same time? She yanked the blankets up around her, trying to protect herself as she fixated on the fog outside her bedroom window. The garden was thick with rain, early morning cloaking the backyard that she played in. It was no longer magic. It was no longer safe.

The bedroom door opened.

Amos rushed in. "Ella?" Sitting on the edge of her bed, he scooped her toward him.

Ella's tremors overtook her as she curled her small body against his chest.

Hugh followed directly behind, flicking on the wall switch for the lamp on her bedside table. "Sweetheart? What's going on?"

She couldn't speak. She wanted to tell them there was something outside. She wanted to warn them it was coming for them. She'd thought more about that sound now: not so much a scream as it was an aria of danger, of expectant dread…

"I think it was just a nightmare," Amos whispered over his shoulder, his hand rubbing her back as she clung to him.

Hugh deflated and took a few steps closer, to put a hand on Amos's shoulder.

Their collective solace seeped into her over the minutes that passed, as her shivers subsided. It was magic, she knew. Amos always knew how to comfort her, how to meld her tears into the background.

Until he didn't.

But that night, he was in control. He put his other hand up on Hugh's as if to channel his partner's strength. "Just a bad dream. Nothing more," he added.

She wanted to believe him. After all, he was one of the smartest people she knew.

Then, Hugh murmured, "But that sound…"

Amos shushed him.

When Ella looked up, her dad was peering out the window toward their backyard. The vein in his neck was strained. She could almost count the pumps of blood coursing through it in the silence as he stayed frozen looking out there.

Amos remained fixated on her. His brow furrowed as he noticed her watching Hugh. "Come on. We'll all sleep together, yeah?"

Hugh broke his gaze from the window and hoisted Ella into his arms. They left her small dark room, navigating the halls where year-round Christmas lights bathed the white walls and wooden accents in warm yellow.

She hid her face in the crook between her dad's neck and shoulder as they passed through the kitchen so she didn't have to look at the patio doors. She imagined a nebulous figure wreathed in the mist at the edge of their property, gray and woolly and able to reach her in a split second…

Then they were in the hallway on the other side of the house. Dozens of pictures of them all together surrounded her like a forcefield of compassion.

Her parents' room was fortified: the walls somehow stronger. Even in the dark, nothing could penetrate it. Nothing could sneak in. Hugh set her down in the bed and pulled the tangle of blankets up over her as she sunk down low into their warmth. Amos leaned in the doorway behind him. For a split second, she saw his eyes flicker to the window on the far side of the room before dropping back on her.

Hugh kissed Ella's cheek as he slid into bed on her left and cupped an arm around her. "Go to sleep, darling. You're safe, I promise."

Moments later, Amos climbed in on her right.

The smell of her dad's sweat on his shirt, the lingering smell of her father's soap, of the fabric softener on the comforter eased her down into a mire of safety. She was on the brink of sleep when she heard Hugh whisper, "I know what I heard, Amos."

"It won't get in," her father was quick to say though it was soft, as if saying the words at all invited the possibility.

"What if it's coming for her?" It was the first time she heard fear in Hugh's tone. Up until then, her parents were never afraid. How could they be with how skilled and powerful they were? And why would they ever need to worry? Everyone loved them…didn't they?

"I won't let it," Amos slid a hand over her head to cup Hugh's cheek. "You won't either."

Hugh kissed his fingers, and Ella heard the echoed promise even though she detected an emptiness in it. Could he not protect her? What weren't they telling her?

Ella faded into sleep, guarded on both sides by her father and her dad, slipped into blank nothingness because nothing was safer than anything in that unidentifiable blip of time between the night and the morning on that most unidentifiable day.

THREE

When she woke, Janet heard the faint strums of a guitar played over a fuzzy radio and opened her eyes to a terrifyingly disturbing thing standing over her: a clown. She pulled back her fist and punched it straight in the mouth as hard as she could.

The Clown collapsed out of sight and fatigue assaulted her. Nothing was clear. Her eyes hurt—how could eyes hurt?—her fingers felt raw and somehow numb. When she passed her hand in front of her face again, she saw bandages on each finger, padding against her ragged flesh from where the witch had torn her nails off at the hotel. Her knuckles were streaked with what looked like black and white and gray paint. Gasping, she bolted up from the cot she lay on.

The Clown held its mouth, make-up smeared around the lips and across the cheek. When he realized she was sitting up, he quickly put up a hand. "No! Don't!"

She started to get to her feet. "Gimme one good reason why I—" Started. Her other wrist stopped her short. It was tied to the metal drawer handle on the other side of the bed. "The hell is this?"

"You're the one who collapsed outside *my* trailer, you loony!" The Clown exclaimed, taking a precautionary stumble back from her. "People are all kinds of crazy these days. You can't trust them. Should have guessed you'd be one of the insane ones." He moaned.

"You'd better untie me right the fuck now or—"

"Or what?" The Clown asked, seeming to have gained a bit of defense back. "You gonna punch me again? If you can reach?"

"Trust me: it won't be a punch." Janet tried to untie the knots but with all the bandages on her fingers, it was impossible to get a good grip. She brought her pointer finger up to her mouth and tried to get her teeth around the end of the medical tape.

"Stop!" The Clown put out a hand. "Don't do that."

"Bite me," she snarled as she finally found an end and started to pull.

"I patched you up because I was trying to help! I'm not trying to hurt you! Look…" The Clown turned toward a small stove with a boiling pot on it. "There's beans and rice here. I was cooking it so you could get some of your energy back."

A stark emotion speared down through her: being alone. The strange swirl of face-paint in front of her was like one she vaguely recollected: one where a mouth stretched open in a hollow of screaming, of crying…

She didn't remember this… When was this? Her throat closed up as panic ignited. She didn't even realize she was half-screaming, "Take the fucking make-up off!"

The Clown scampered around a corner out of sight in the tiny space. A faucet squeaked on seconds before a torrent of water splurged into a sink. "I'm taking it off!" he called through the swishing of water. Moments later, when he reappeared, the face-paint was faded and streaky and made him look paler than a ghost. She saw his pointed nose, his large green eyes, his smile and suddenly he was a human again.

"See? Not a psycho. Not going to kill you…"

Janet took a deep breath through her nose. "Can you please untie me?"

The Clown carefully slid a knife from the butcher block on the counter nearby. "Promise you won't hurt me?"

Reluctantly, Janet nodded.

The Clown hesitantly reached over her and sawed through the rope holding her to the drawer handle. It took longer than either of them expected; the Clown's back and forth pull becoming exaggerated as the seconds ticked by. Janet did her best to keep her frustration in check.

Once freed, she rubbed her wrist and became a human Swiss Army Knife: body compact, ready to unfold into fury if she needed to. But she was already beginning to feel like that was unnecessary. That and the exhaustion had caught up with her almost as quickly as the pain. She was in terrible shape and wasn't going to make it to Steele without time to recoup. She wasn't even sure how long she'd been out of commission since getting off the train.

The Clown picked two bowls from the nearby cabinet and spooned giant helpings of gloppy rice and beans into them before handing one to Janet with a spoon. She dug in greedily. A stray thought hit her that he could have poisoned it—but why go to the trouble of fixing her up?—and soon enough, he ate from his own helping.

Janet studied his face, the only sound between them the

plinking spoons. Black make-up still shadowed his eyes, and made them look like cavernous hollows for his green irises to sit inside. Now that she realized it, his whole costume was closer to a skeleton than it was a clown. His figure was slight and string-beany, large hands and feet accentuated by ridiculously long shoes and gloves with fingers that seemed far too long to be real. Big ears and a prominent Adam's apple. Short shaggy brown hair. Hard to say what his age was with the off-gray tone of his skin but he seemed young; he might not have been much older than her.

He put the spoon down, chewing his food. "My name is—"

"I don't want to know," she cut him off.

The Clown stared at his bowl. "Fine. I won't ask your name either."

"It's Janet."

He winced. "Well, that doesn't seem fair now, does it?"

"I don't care who knows. In fact…" She let an eyebrow spring up toward her hairline. "I want that son of a bitch to know I'm coming for him."

"What son of a bitch gets that pleasure?"

"Steele."

She didn't think it was possible for the Clown to go paler, but she was mistaken. His sights shifted around the trailer as if there were gremlins hiding in its nooks and crannies before he scrunched his neck down into his shoulders. It made him look like some hunchback that should have been swinging around in towers, not cowering in a cramped trailer.

"The Most Esteemed Guest of Honor," he practically spit the words as if they tasted bad. "He used to frequent our carnival quite a bit."

Janet perked up. Maybe this clown wasn't so useless after all. Maybe this was a way for her to get at Steele without exposing herself too much. "What changed?" she asked.

"He got bored of it," he said. "Centurion Fair hasn't exactly taken on any new and interesting acts in the last several years. Though…" He put a finger to his chin. "There was that one man who said he could make his pecs, nipples, and penis dance to the Macarena—It was such a let down!—And that woman that said she could talk with beavers. Oh, that would have killed!"

Janet read between the lines, her hopes sagging. "So, you haven't seen him in a while?"

He began to shake his head but then his eyes lit up and a brilliant smile jumped onto his face. "Oh! I heard we were doing a special show tomorrow night though. Rex said—he's my boss—that St… The Most Esteemed Guest of Honor, that is…bought out the tent. Suppose he's bringing in a new pack of thralls; that's what he calls them. Wants to keep their wonder satisfied and their wallets empty."

Janet shook her head. "I don't understand."

The Clown's gaze dropped to a point on the rug. "Nothingland is the end. Didn't you know that? There's nothing after this. It's like…what if people chose to blind themselves with manufactured happiness so they could forget all the awful things they've seen? All the terrible things they've done? This place kind of holds you on its tongue, tasting you, letting you dissolve, but never bites down. There's no quick end here."

Janet hadn't realized she was holding her breath and when she let it out, it shook out of her like sheet left on a wash-line before a storm. She felt lightheaded as she asked, "And Steele?"

"He bankrolls it. Not that this place would ever run out of money or indulgences for people to get their titties in a twist about. You remember Pinocchio? That place where all the bad little boys got shipped off to so they could break glass and smoke cigars and be obnoxious little wankers?"

Janet nodded. It never was her favorite Disney film.

"Well, that's Nothingland. There's all manner of ways to act out or disappear or whatever. And no one leaves. It just keeps going back into the same cycle over and over." The Clown hung his head and mumbled. "Pretty sure that son of a bitch gets off on other people's misery."

Looking around the trailer, Janet zeroed in on a variety of childlike drawings taped to the fake wood paneling, the tiny metal mobiles hanging from the ceiling with various zoo animals: zebras, tigers, elephants... She got the impression he'd grown up here. That the circus was his home and had been for some time. Still, she asked, "Why do you stay? If this place is as bad as you say it is?"

"Because this carnival is my home and these people—freaks the lot of them—are my family. I feel safer with them than out there."

Ah yes. The metaphorical 'Out There' that Janet could picture beyond the back wall of the small trailer: a world filled with struggling cities run by the opportunistic dirt-clods that populated the skyscrapers and expensive town houses, condos, private manors... They didn't care about what was once the middle and lower classes even if that's what they unceremoniously leapt into their stations of power from.

The homeless staked out the sturdiest-looking tarps and plastic bins to shelter in at overpasses, tunnels, and bridges. Camps of miserable wretches who clustered and drove anyone who wasn't inside out.

Kindness had been replaced with survival in its most boiled-down sense. Janet hadn't seen a lick of it since her time with the traveling community that used to set up outside her hometown. She'd left them because their desire to fight back against oppression had faded. Looking back now, she recognized how much of a naïve little brat she'd been in their company, content to be an upstart, to flit around between the ruined flotsam and jetsam of what was once the USA as long as there was fire inside of her that never went out. Anger was all she'd known. But it had cost her. It had cost others.

Still, she found the Clown's statement ignorant and rolled her eyes at it. "You live on the edge of a fucking hypnotist's spiral, dude."

His smile disappeared. "I'm not like those lost people out there."

"Whatever," Janet exhaled.

"I helped you!" He waved at the bandages on her fingers. "Do you think anyone from Out There would have done that for you?"

She shrugged.

"Fine." He picked up his bowl and fed the spoon in again for another mouthful, all the while talking through it. "If that's how you feel, you can take that attitude and shove off. Go and try to kill the guest of honor just like all those other stupid people."

Whatever bravado Janet had at the start of their conversation hissed out like a sputtering candle flame with his words. "What other people?"

He squinted at her. "You thought you were the first?" He stood up, plopped his bowl and spoon on the counter and gave a wave of his hand. "Come on."

They left the trailer. The winter air cut Janet's skin with its razor cold.

The Clown barely acknowledged it, only burrowing his head further into his floppy sweater and crossing his arms over his chest as he trudged through the gathering of trailers toward a hill at the edge of camp.

Janet followed numbly. She studied the small lights in the various trailers around them, heard the muffled laughs and conversations happening within. They climbed the hill side-by-side, boots slipping in the dead grass there as they scaled its near vertical slope. At the top, the Clown waved his hand toward a series of deep hollows in the land. "There they are: the Pits."

For the first time since she was a girl, Janet felt small. The land stretched for a good two or three miles before it reached the lights and grandeur of Steele's Nothingland, highlighted on the horizon in a varying array of neon lights and colors. In between. Rows and rows of dark gray trenches plowed through the landscape. From higher above, she imagined it might look like something had tilled the land there, trying to turn it into a farm. But the trenches were deep and sewn with bodies. Arms with skeletal hands popped against the black soil, bits of cloth, mangled faces with lost stares, broken jaws and noses, skin scraped or rotted away over time stretching for miles and miles.

FOUR

J anet inspected the pits, the darkness the bodies... Tossed inside without a care of who they were, what they'd lost, how far they'd come to exact revenge, to feel a flicker of acceptance or relief in their souls... Nothing of their identities or their struggle was left. If she wasn't careful, she'd end up just like them.

They retreated back to the safety of the circus and the clown's trailer. She noticed how he relaxed once they were out of the wind and suppressed a shiver as she, too, eased into the close, dare she even admit, cozy room.

The Clown helped himself to another bowl of food and perched on the bench seat opposite her. "If you keep your eyes on the train yard over the hill, there's bound to be a freighter heading out in the next day or so. You could be on it without...him even knowing you got here."

"I can't do that."

The Clown clicked his tongue. "That's your funeral then."

"This is probably a long-shot, but do you know anyone that goes by 'The Junco' here?"

A smile unfurled on the Clown's face. "Oh, yeah. *Everyone*

knows her."

Janet's attention prickled. "What's with the tone?"

"She runs the Garden of Delights: most popular drug den in town."

Drug den? Janet's lip threatened to curl. Almost every hollow in every city had become an Eden for drugs Out There. Janet had cowered in places for the night, hoping to catch up on sleep and known she was sharing space with people who were seeing things she would never see, riding the lightning bolt of pain and pleasure. People who had wrapped themselves in addictive oblivion so that they could feel some echo of the joy they once knew.

"There's no one else?" Janet caught herself before her impatience sprouted. "I mean... Are you sure?"

"About as sure as I know our resident cyclops, Begonia, only has one eye." The Clown must have caught something in Janet's gaze because he was very quick to add, "Accident with a fork."

Shit. Why the hell would Hugh have told her to partner up with a drug supplier? Especially one as well-known in Nothingland as this Junco character? Maybe they had information about Steele's movements that could help get Janet close? And a smaller niggling question that bit at the back of her tongue with every moment that had passed since Hugh's death: what had their relationship been? Close enough that he trusted the Junco with his own daughter, trusted them with the plan to kill Steele?

"How do I get there?" she asked hesitantly.

"I mean..." The Clown scratched his scruffy hair. "It's not like we've got street names or anything. Suppose I could draw you a map but that would take time…"

"I've already wasted enough time sleeping—"

"You mean healing?"

"He probably already knows I'm here."

The Clown stared at the ground. He stared for so long that Janet almost wanted to ask him if he was suffering some kind of aneurysm before he said, "I could show you."

Was he serious? Janet blinked a few times. God, he was. Fear was an invisible force projected from his stare that she felt every ounce of, heavy enough to make her grunt.

No. She didn't want that. She didn't want that responsibility latched onto her when she was in the devil's territory. The Clown had already helped her enough. If she made him do this, he'd be putting himself at risk of becoming one of those bodies in the pits.

No. With her luck, he *would* be.

So, she shook her head. "It's fine. Make me the map."

It was nearly an hour later before the Clown handed her something that reminded her of a tic-tac-toe board, but with more lines. A series of arrows pointed her from a triangle to a big X in the top left corner. Some chicken scratch handwriting accompanied it but Janet could hardly decipher each word let alone each letter. How could someone with such artistic skill, as advertised by the drawings all over the trailer, not be able to form words better than a first-grader? To be fair, Janet couldn't remember the last time she wrote something down on paper. The last time she wrote anything was with a pen and a lighter as she carved her father's words into her forearm.

She peeled back the gauze from the tattoo on her forearm. It was still red but less so than when she last looked at it. The words ceded her resolve though. She wished Amos were here to give her advice on how to proceed, wished Hugh was there to help her bury her lingering skepticism about the Junco.

Before she left, the Clown offered her clothes from his costume closet: a wool trench coat that shielded the backs of her legs from the wind along with a sweater with a hood that she could put up over her head underneath her winter cap.

The Clown walked her out toward the edge of the carnival. They passed the cage with the enormous cat which had settled along the floor, its paws occasionally prodding and pulsing the air as if it were a kitten kneading for milk. She caught the Clown's smile and watched as he stopped and talked to the creature. "You cheeky bum. You're so sly, you know that? Always looking like you've gotten away with something while I'm not looking."

The lion's growl smoldered from somewhere deep in its stomach.

"How dangerous is it?" Janet asked, feeling stupid for the question. It was a fucking lion. It should be prowling through tall grass with more of its kind, maybe casually chewing on the head of an antelope or something. It didn't belong here.

"Sammy's trained. Been with the circus since she was a wee little lady. She wouldn't harm a hair on anyone's head here unless she were defending herself. You, though? Not so sure. Then, well… I wouldn't want to see the fucker who tried anything."

The Clown walked her to the lights. When she looked back at him, she noted his frown. "I'd hate to see you in one of those pits, Janet. Don't underestimate the Most Esteemed Guest of Honor."

Janet gave the Clown a once over from his silly shoes to his baggy pants, his tattered and pilled sweater to his soft, streaked shadow face. "He's the one who underestimated me. It'll be the last fucking mistake he ever makes."

She turned and started on foot toward Nothingland.

FIVE

The hospice center was a flutter when Ella and her dad visited that oddly cold spring day. Nurses, gathered at their various stations, whispered amongst themselves. If they weren't whispering, they were staring. Each set of eyes that fell on her was like a cold drop of rain rolling down her scalp. She didn't like them. She didn't understand what was so interesting about her and Hugh.

But then, she overheard it: the on-call nurse from her father's floor uttering in her slightest voice to her dad that Amos had "had a rough morning." When Hugh tried to ask for details, the nurse eyed Ella. Taking the hint, Hugh sat her down in the waiting area a few feet away and handed her one of the magazines on the table.

As Ella stared at the bright photo of the family gathered on their spacious deck, smiling their plastic smiles and showing off their starched, pastel clothes, she wondered why this hospice place couldn't let them stay with Amos while they made him better.

Their home felt so empty without him there. There was no longer any Fleetwood Mac percolating from the turntable in the kitchen first thing in the morning. No more of his poems about the stars or the flowers in their garden at bed time. When she made a mistake in her drawings, he wasn't there to fix them. When she wanted to dance, she didn't have a partner.

And Hugh tried. He tried to fill in where he could but… he couldn't do it all.

When Hugh came to retrieve her from the waiting room, she recognized the tear tracks on his cheeks, the dark wet stain at the end of his sleeve where he'd wiped them away. "It's going to be a short visit today, Ella. Amos isn't feeling very good, so we don't want to upset him too much, okay?"

"Why did that lady say he had a rough morning?"

Hugh's eyes darted around. He took her hand and carefully led her down the hall toward the elevator. When she looked back over her shoulder, she noticed another couple sitting in the waiting room beside her now speaking in hushed tones. Once inside the elevator, Hugh squeezed her hand. "It's harder for Amos now, Ella. You remember how we talked about how he's forgetting things? How he can't help it? Well, he forgot where he was this morning and it frightened him."

Ella remembered a time when she'd tried to spend the night at a friend's house; the first time she had spent a night away from her parents. She'd awoken in the quiet darkness, not in her own bed and with a room that smelled faintly like potpourri. She couldn't hear the grass in the meadow behind her home, couldn't hear the night sounds of the creatures in the woods. She'd cried and yelled for her parents. And approximately twenty minutes after she'd awoken, Hugh had arrived to take her home.

Except they weren't here to take Amos home today. He was going to have to stay here with all these strange people until they could make him better. She didn't like that at all.

Hugh, as if noticing her expression, patted her shoulder. "We'll cheer him up. Won't we?"

She nodded.

The elevator dinged and the doors parted to the painfully white hallway. Even as they stepped off and started toward Amos's room, Ella had made up her mind. She wasn't going to let her father go. She wanted to stay with him. She didn't want him to be alone anymore. If she never let him go, Hugh would let her stay. The doctors wouldn't be able to part them. They could all stay together.

The door to the second room from the end of the hall's was open. Inside, Amos sat in the armchair near the window frowning. One of his pajama pant legs was scrunched halfway up his leg to the knee, the other down. His eyes were full of red scattering from the tear ducts toward his irises while beneath them were puffed violet-colored bags. She'd never seen him like this and wondered for a brief moment if they'd replaced him, if they were trying to fool her and her dad with a *thing* that looked and sounded like Amos…

The moment they were inside, Amos eyed them suspiciously. "Excuse me?"

"Amos, we're here to visit you," Hugh said, his voice soft and filled with hesitance.

The specter in the shape of her father exhaled. He tapped each finger with his thumb as if counting them to make sure they were all still there. "I think you might have the wrong room."

A joke. He was playing. Ella remembered when he used to do this when she was little. He'd pretend he couldn't see her when she was right in front of him, as if she had magically gone invisible. All pretend. They'd laugh as he'd find her and tickle her. She wasn't sure that was what was happening.

Hugh's expression was bleached of any humor at all. Maybe he knew it wasn't Amos either.

Still, she had to check.

"Daddy?" she asked Amos, creeping around Hugh's legs.

And her father's entire disorientation crumpled in an instant at the sight of her. His eyes welled up with tears, his mouth quivered and his hands shook so hard, she worried he was going to slip right out of his skin. He reached for her and she let him fold her into his embrace.

"I'm sorry," he murmured. "I'm so sorry I couldn't protect you."

When she looked up over Amos's shoulder, she could see Hugh's expression contorted in confusion. "Amos?"

"We can't save her!" Amos babbled. "It's coming."

Before she understood what was happening, she felt herself being pried out of Amos's grip and the chill envelop her once his touch was gone. Something had been warming her, settling into her from his embrace, something that tingled under her skin like embers in a growing fire. But now, she was on her own, standing somewhere in the emptiness between the chair and the bed and the door. Amos clung to Hugh like a drowning man to a life preserver, wailing and sputtering, her dad calmly stroking his back and shushing him.

"It was here…" Amos cried. "She was here… I saw her out there… Heard her…"

"Darling, you're confused. It was just a nurse coming to help you get dressed. It's okay."

"No! I saw her! *Her!*"

More people came into the room. Men and women in white, one who bumped into Ella and didn't apologize, maybe didn't even notice. "Sir, sir! You should leave," one of them advised as they muscled their way in between her dads.

Upset bubbled in Ella with the sight, seeing them put their hands on her father, seeing them separate her parents like that. Even as it spilled out of her, Hugh's hands settled on her shoulders, trying to lift her and put her into his arms. But she started screaming. She wasn't sure what.

"Get me out of here!" Amos was crying. "Please!"

Tears flowed hot down her cheeks. Her blood boiled and her skin sizzled… How could they touch him like that? How dare they do this to him!

Hugh's face was suddenly in hers, shouting her name, his hands firm on her arms. Her sound dried up, the anger along with it as if being leeched from her. In moments, she melted into her father's arms and sobbed.

In Amos's room behind them, a nurse had calmed her father down, had given him something for his nerves. He was sitting almost as he'd been when they first walked in, as if nothing had happened at all. "Pretty view," she heard him murmur. He was looking out his window. "Very striking."

SIX

Janet followed the power line corridor through the dried-up weeds, amidst the bristling red thorn patches beside the pits for the dead. At first, she was determined not to look, not to let what she had seen already influence her in any way, shape or form. After all, she had somewhere to be. Something to do. Someone to kill.

But as the walk dragged on and on and the pits along with them, that little voice of doubt inside her head that had cozied up beside the mounting pain from her various injuries pulled her attention from the path ahead to the odes of death below.

One look was all it took.

She suddenly found herself on the ground, howling, fighting the urge to puke because what she'd seen—oh holy fuck—what she'd just seen… Corpses of all sizes lined those pits. Corpses in all stages of decomposition. In all colors. In all genders. Whole. In pieces. Dirt covered. Nude. Clothed. And faces. Why was it faces that she'd had to focus on?

Countless.

Teeth. No teeth. Eyes. One eye. No eyes. No nose. The scraped remains of one. The flesh looked like it had been dragged across pavement, bits of skin curled and flaked like loose bits from carpet.

She swallowed it down. And crawled forward until she could stand. She shuffled until she could walk. She walked until she could run.

This fucker needed to die. Today.

She'd pictured the Garden of Delights to be something discreet, one of those dens that was unassuming from the outside: maybe a brick façade with a tiny sign over a doorway down a dimly lit alley? But no. She'd followed the Clown's directions carefully, making sure that once she was within the city limits, she stuck to the shadows and embraced anonymity with the help of her new disguise from the Clown's closet.

What awaited her at the X on the map was a sleek granite building, the outside sheathed in polished black marble with a large window looking into a hot pink realm. Golden metal letters over the entrance invited anyone who dared to enter the Garden.

But where she'd expected to see a horde of people clambering for their next fix, instead, she found what appeared to be several leather couches, monsteras, palms, spider plants, cactuses and ivy dripping from terracotta pots all throughout the room. Moss rimmed candlesticks glowed beside a large fountain with a black-looking pond beneath it, all bathed in that strange magenta hue. And gardens. Gardens sprawled as far back as the eye-could-see and people sprawled amongst them.

Was it a drug den or a Chinese Food restaurant? She wasn't sure anymore. And she wasn't sure if she should take the risk of walking in the front door. But what other choice did she have? She needed answers. If the Junco had maintained their notoriety in the wake of Steele's omnipresence, surely there would be a safe space for them to discuss taking him out.

Janet pulled back the heavy glass door and walked in. It was warm. Too warm. Like being inside of a greenhouse. The air was thick and heady with the sweet scents of various blossoms and almost immediately, Janet found herself sweating beneath the heavy layers. A passing thought hit her—she'd rushed into the hotel back in Town in search of Steele and had completely blown through a spell set on the front doors by the Witch. It had cost her her fingernails.

Had she done that again?

She was unprepared: no herbs in her bag, only her trusty wrench (cleaned thanks to the Clown who admitted to her that he gagged half a dozen times whilst doing so). But there was enough magic brimming in her blood for her to take a deep breath and focus—just like Hugh had taught her.

"Just focus."

There was nothing on the doors. There was, however, a corona of starlight emanating from the plants in the endless garden near the fountain, enough so that it almost drowned out the pink of the lights. When she was close enough to examine them for herself, Janet understood why.

Bright pink poppies with yellow centers that stared at her like eyes were set amongst the tall green Salvia stalks with violet petals. Clusters of red Betel Nut leaves hung from planters above, raining down toward white siphon-esque blossoms of Jimsonweed, pots of cacti including the small spherical pale green of—

"Mescaline. Is that something you can get around here?" she heard Amos say in her mind.

"You're about a thousand miles away from any Peyote."

She'd been wrong.

Janet was staring at a sea of psychoactive plants, a garden of mind-altering bliss that stretched from her to the purple darkness of the back wall. And in between her and that wall were nearly twenty people lounging amidst the leaves and bright petals, deep in whatever herbal cocktail they'd been dosed with. Several writhed as though they'd become snakes, their bodies twisting and reaching for the candles or the pink neon as if they were thirsty and reaching for water.

"I know what you're thinking," someone said, catching Janet's attention from the back of the room. "What a pitiful sight. But if you're here, it must be because you want to be just like them."

In the dusky shadows, Janet noticed a lectern stationed by a heavily tattooed young woman with wild mahogany hair. Her rosy lips turned up at Janet as she reached the counter and said, "The Garden of Delights welcomes whoever wants to bask for however long. I'll be your Guide. All you need to do is pick out which infusion you'd like and we can find you a place to lay."

It was tempting. The thought of casting all her inhibitions aside if only to actually enjoy something, even if that joy wasn't for anything real. When was the last time she experienced true joy? She couldn't remember. The snapshots of days gone by could have been from any year but the last one with her parents. All the beautiful birthdays, planting in their garden, watching stars, dancing, eating strawberry shortcake… Lost under a deluge of pain and sadness and anger… So much anger…

It could be turned off with a deep breath of—she looked at the menu—Narcissus Bliss or Holy Myristicin Delirium.

The Guide's smile was eerily the same when she looked back up. "What'll it be?"

Janet crossed her arms. "I'm looking for the Junco."

The Guide blinked almost robotically. "She's not taking clients right now."

"Tell her Hugh sent me." She added under her breath. "She'll want to talk to me."

Squinting, the Guide picked up a phone on the desk and pressed a button. Janet wasn't sure how she managed to speak so quietly as to not be heard. Maybe it was because her attention was pulled back to toward the languishing bodies in the garden. It reminded her of that scene from *The Wizard of Oz* where Dorothy fell asleep in the poppies.

She heard her dad's voice. *"Stay focused."*

The phone hung up behind her. She turned to look at the Guide.

"She wants to see you. Right this way." The Guide led her toward what appeared to be a black wall and brushed a barely noticeable curtain aside to reveal an elevator. With a push of a button, the doors sliced open to reveal a red interior.

Danger.

Red.

Danger.

Janet stepped in after her, forcing her instinctive alarms down into the shuffle of her thoughts. She'd already made herself known. No reason to cut and run yet.

They rode up in silence. No music. Nothing but the sound of the cable shifting above them.

"You take that shit down there?" Janet asked before she could help it. "That Narcissus Bliss?"

The Guide side-eyed her. The shock in her sapphire eyes was one that Janet didn't anticipate. "Sometimes it helps me sleep."

All at once, Janet remembered the Clown's words. Remembered why people seek out Nothingland. Why they come and never leave. Shame crowded in on her for the rest of the ride.

The elevator stopped and the doors opened to a long black hallway, lit only by horizontal strips of orange light along the walls. As the Guide led her further into the dark, Janet's hand curled around the wrench head and tried to discern what her best strategy would be if the Guide suddenly turned on her here.

The thought didn't make it past its inception before the outline of a door emerged in the blackness ahead of them. The Guide knocked once before opening it and stepping through. Janet tentatively followed; hand still poised for action above her father's wrench.

A vast office opened up ahead of her, the floor carpeted in midnight blue while a tall, angled set of windows overlooked the streets outside in Nothingland, its endless gleam of lights and the sky behind them fading from violet to black.

Standing behind the desk was a woman with short dark

hair, curled at her forehead in a luxurious up-do. She wore a black velveteen blazer over her bronze sheathed dress, bold dark red lipstick and a flash of emerald green eyeshadow.

The Junco.

In her hand was a gun.

Janet stilled.

In one fluent motion, the Junco raised the weapon in her direction and fired.

SEVEN

Janet closed her eyes on instinct moments before she heard the bullet kiss its mark with the tear of flesh and heard the sound of her Guide's body crumpling onto the carpet in front of her. When she opened them again, she was entreated to the sight of a growing blood pool and the Guide's shocked blue eyes fluttering before going still.

Janet scoured the room.

She needed to hide.

To run.

But she couldn't make herself move.

How could she outrun a bullet?

The Junco set the gun down on the desk in front of her with a clatter and reached for a joint lying in a small ceramic tray to take a hit. "It's a shame," she said. Her voice dragged a little at the end and reminded Janet of a woman from an old-time film noir. What had Amos called them? Femme Fatales.

The Junco kept speaking. "She was one of my best guides. But you gave her a name that can't be spoken around here. She'd have taken it straight to Him. You understand why I had to do it, don't you?"

Janet nodded. Her dad's name. "I said it in front of a bunch of your patrons downstairs."

The Junco scoffed. "None of them were even awake enough to comprehend it. We've done our due diligence for now." She waved at the chair in front of the desk. "Come have a seat."

The spell of immobility broken, Janet approached the desk and eyed the seat. "I feel better standing, thanks."

"Whatever your preference, sweetie," The Junco said. "You look like you could use a rest but who am I to tell a fellow lady what she needs." She plopped in to the plush swivel chair on her side of the desk. "Nice jacket. Feel like I've seen it somewhere before."

Her words were fishing. She recognized the bait on the end of the cast question right away. "A friend let me borrow it."

The Junco's brow arched before she tented her hands on the desk and leaned forward a little. "Is he dead? Hugh?"

The words made her dad's last moments resurface momentarily in her head: the scissors, the feeling of blood gushing through her fingers as she knelt over his body… She tried to clear her throat to no avail. Instead, she nodded.

The Junco stared at the glossy surface of her desk, indifference a mask on her face. It slid, but only for a moment. Janet saw the sadness before she covered it up again. "I'd ask how but I don't think it matters. We're all bound to end up in the same grave someday."

A nihilistic viewpoint but for Janet, hope was nothing but smoke vanishing from the extinguished candle anyway.

She figured if she'd lived in a place like Nothingland for more than a week, she'd probably share the same jaded outlook as the Junco.

A spark inside of her, however tiny, told her she had a chance of making it out of this place. Maybe she'd wind up back at that ludicrous circus. Start over. Bring dead things back to life under the Big Top for applause and some weird form of acceptance.

"You know," The Junco started, pulling Janet's attention back to the matter at hand. "I never met anyone quite like Hugh. Plenty of others who could do some shitty sorcery, some even toting their wicked talents for all the wrong reasons. But he withheld his true power. You could smell it coming off of him: like a pie right out of the oven. Completely immaculate on top but boiling inside."

Janet hated the description, her dad reduced to a sumptuous piece of food. But she kept quiet, even if she wanted to walk away right then and there. This wasn't the time for her emotions to take the reins.

"He didn't deny it," The Junco added, taking another puff. "But he said he couldn't do what he used to, not without his husband. They shared in their magic: some type of family bond, I suppose. I heard he died rather tragically. Hugh would never talk about it but I think it cracked the top of his crust, if you catch my drift."

Janet's gaze hardened into a glare. "How *exactly* did you two know each other?"

The Junco cocked her head. "I figured he'd have told you."

"There wasn't enough time." Not exactly the truth but she wasn't about to reveal that she was the one who dug the scissors into Hugh's chest. And every time the thought came up to the brim of her mind, she'd scurry to quash it back down. His eyes. His eyes just…

"He used to frequent my establishment a lot when he was in the city."

This time, Janet couldn't hold in her distaste. "Is that right?"

"As it turns out, he had a wonderful green thumb. He never came here to partake; only to put his hands into the dirt every now and again. Help cultivate. Hugh broke a lot of things and people in his time with Steele. I think growing things made him feel whole again."

Janet bit her gums. She'd felt the same, for a time, after she'd lost Amos in the marten's body. But that connection had been broken almost as soon as it had started. She wondered if she'd ever find it again. "So," she said. "You two became friendly and got your hands dirty."

The Junco watched Janet, her eyes narrowing. "In spite of the fact that Hugh was a killer, it never absolved him of his desire for genuine empathy or companionship, just like all humans need. Yes: we became *friendly*. We became *friends*. We trusted one another. Which is why you're here."

Janet nodded. "He told me you could help me kill Steele."

The Junco's eyebrows perked. "Ah. Yes. It is death you're after." She stood up from the seat and left the joint sitting on the tray as she stepped over to the window that overlooked Nothingland. Her faint, mirrored reflection gazed back at her from the blue void of night. "I can help you. But it's going to cost you."

"I don't have anything to offer you," Janet was quick to say.

The Junco scoffed. "What did you expect when you got

here? That I'd just give you whatever you wanted for nothing? I don't know you and information like this is pricey. It's my life and livelihood at stake here."

She had a point. Of course she did. But Janet was about as messed up as a tuft of grass from beneath a lawnmower. Everything still ached mercilessly, even with the fever gone. The Clown had done what little he could to cover her wounds but she could see the red leaking out from beneath the rudimentary bandages. Shortly after leaving, she'd taken every single one off her fingers. In the cold, they were raw and screamed to be covered once more.

"What then?" she asked.

The Junco crossed the room from the window to a map pinned on the wall amongst a sea of other notes and cards on a cork board. She waved at Janet to come closer and once she had, placed her finger in the upper right-hand corner of the tangle of roads. "There's a church at the edge of Nothingland. In its graveyard, they grow a plant that I've been wanting to cultivate here at the Garden. There's not a lot of it, mind you, so you'll need to take care in bringing it back. Once you've retrieved it, then I'll tell you what you want to know."

"What plant?" Janet frowned. "And why can't you go get it yourself?"

"Nothingland is made up of the Four Corners of Odiousness. The Carnival lays claim to the south east, my Garden to the North West, the Casinos in the South West and the Church in the North East. We have rules: citizens of Nothingland can waltz wherever they please, play pinball between the various sins but for those of us who run each corner… Well, we're meant to remain where we've been put."

"Like a King on a chessboard," Janet murmured. She'd played against Amos a handful of times as a girl but she could never memorize how each piece moved. What she did know was that if her King or Queen ever got surrounded, she had lost. It happened several times before she got mad and didn't want to play anymore.

"Right," the Junco said. "I can't leave the Garden. And the Graveyard isn't exactly part of the attractions offered in the realm of the Church."

A graveyard at an old church. Why bother with a graveyard when they had pits for miles that they could just dump all their nameless bodies into when they were done with them? And a church in Nothingland? Janet wondered exactly what kind of awfulness she would find there.

"What plant is it?" she asked again.

"Wild Strawberries."

A memory. Amos washing strawberries in their sink at home. Accidentally staining one of her crude drawings. The sadness in his eyes.

And her ingenuity to turn that red smear into a fox.

"This is the best time for me to plant them, you see. If you bring me back a plant with the roots, it'll overwinter nicely in a pot here in my office. If you're only able to bring back the berries, I can plant the seeds but it's a more finicky process. For either of these, I'll give you what you want."

Janet sighed. She was never an errand girl. Bartering was the economy now though and she had nothing else she could offer this woman. Even though Hugh had trusted her, Janet didn't want to give her too much information, particularly that she and Hugh were related.

Steele had wanted Janet's power as a child; it was the reason Hugh had done what he had, made her believe he was dead, made her take refuge with the caravan. So far, no one knew who she was or exactly why she was in Nothingland and if she could keep it that way up until she buried her father's wrench in Steele's skull, she would.

"Fine," she agreed. "I'll get your berries for you."

The Junco nodded, a pleased smile pulling at her lips. "Lovely. Shall I tell you what they look like?"

"I know." Janet scoffed. "You see them almost everywhere where I'm from."

The Junco's brows rose. "I'm envious."

"Don't be." She shook her head. "It's the same as everywhere else."

Giving a nod, the Junco walked Janet over to the window and pointed toward the far side of Nothingland. A spire with a pointed roof jutted up over some brick buildings in the distance. She thought she caught sight of stained glass but wasn't sure. "That's the church. Mass will be starting in about an hour. If you wait until everyone is inside, you can probably find a plant and get out without being noticed."

"Is there any reason to suspect I could find it anywhere else on the property?" Janet asked. "After all, a graveyard seems very specific for something that typically spreads aggressively?"

The Junco cocked her head. "You know your plants."

"Like I said, I'm familiar with them."

"The Church tends the yard. In the winter, they'll harvest them make strawberry wine for their ceremonies. I hope it hasn't already happened."

"And if it has?"

"Then you'll have to find a berry inside to bring back."

"And if I'm caught?"

The Junco sighed. "Then we don't know each other. This conversation never happened. And, you'll want to find the best way to off yourself if you can."

Great. Janet turned toward the office doors.

"My guide told me your name was Janet. Is that right?" The Junco called to her.

Looking back over her shoulder, Janet nodded.

"Beware the Mother Superior. She likes fresh meat."

Without a sound, Janet fled the office for the hall, skin rapidly cooling at the darkness that closed around her and with the thought of what awaited her at the Church.

EIGHT

Rain. It hadn't rained in such a long time. But there it was, deep in the night, deep in the dark. She knew she should wake up Hugh, tell him they needed to get their canteens and jars out to collect whatever they could before it was over. But he'd only fallen asleep about ten minutes ago. She could tell by the evenness of his breaths and the absence of his crying.

The hiss of the water's percussion called to her as she shimmied out of her sleeping bag and found her father's old backpack leaning against the ice-cold wall of the train-tunnel. His giant travel mug slid silently from the side pocket into her little hands. Though she was tempted to open it right then, she knew the metal lid would shriek under the tension.

No, she told herself. *Get outside. Do it there.*

Finding her own pink unicorn bottle and scuttling out from under the blue tarp, Ella stood for a moment in the gloom of early morning, the arch of the tunnel's entrance only ten feet away. Curtains of rain fell on the world outside, feeding the dried, hungry earth. The countryside beyond was bathed in darkness, in a mist that hid its brittle grass and hills for miles.

Ella moved so as not to wake anyone else between their camp and the tunnel's entrance; at least another five were set up, some with lamplight clearly showing them and others nothing more than heavy plastic suspended oddly over bodies. Her boot accidentally caught on the strap from someone's cheap tent but she was quick to recover and not a single person inside stirred.

She made it to the border between dry and wet and cautiously unscrewed the caps of both bottles. Her father's cap stuck and she had to use the sleeve of her shirt to help wrench it open. Any sound it might have made was drowned by the water pounding on the track ballast. She set each bottle out amongst the downpour and watching the cascade of rain spatter against the tips of her plastic rain boots. She wanted to stand in it. She wanted to be swallowed in its beauty, rub the dirt and the sweat from her skin, let it course through her hair, thick with knots. She probably should have woken someone else. They all deserved to get as much of this as they could.

But she remained quiet. She stuck her hand out and let the drops beat on her skin, slide over the lines in her palm and between her fingers.

The scream pierced her, its cry bombarding her like the resounding of a faraway animal as it hunted. Goosebumps formed all over her, her cheeks coloring and her stomach leaping as the sound died away.

She knew it. She remembered that sound.

Last time she'd heard it, she was safe in her bed or at least she'd thought so at the time, Amos and Hugh rushing into protect her. Now…

Now she was out here *with* it. Nothing but a flimsy tarp and the thin synthetic of her sleeping bag to keep its claws from slicing…

There. Ella blinked and for a moment, something at the edge of the field nearby made its presence known: a dark smudge at the corner of her vision. But when she tried to look at it head-on, it would shift to another corner, the grass left sweeping from its movement.

Breath caught in her throat, Ella took a step back into the darkness of the tunnel. Maybe it hadn't seen her? Maybe if she could tip-toe back to her bed, back to where Hugh was resting, she'd be safe.

Amos's words came to her then: *"There, there. It's nothing but a bad dream."*

Thinking about him twisted her insides. The pain exploded as she glimpsed every snapshot in her head of her father: of his smile, of his laugh, of the way he hugged her goodnight, of the way he spoke, and dressed and the manner of him all from before…

And now he was gone.

He was gone *forever*.

Ella dropped on her hands and knees, choking back the sobs, her body bucking with each one.

The cries released from her in primordial yowls, leaving her a gaping maw. The wailing pinged against the stones in the tunnel, pummeled against her bones, radiating from her pores.

Her father was dead. He couldn't protect her anymore.

Her blood simmered, her pulse thrumming against her

flesh. Her loss was a song. She needed to get it out. She needed to let it soar.

A long shadow fell over her like a curtain being closed. She stared up at the shape, at the silhouetted statuesque thing standing over her, its head swallowed in a wreath of hair, eyes vast holes, mouth parted and—keening.

Her voice and its voice: harmonizing in torturous despair. In the screams of loss. In the screams of desolation.

Ella didn't remember closing her eyes, didn't remember her mouth ever closing or her thoughts of Amos ever winnowing. When she woke though, Hugh had her in his arms. His hair matted by rain. His clothes soaked. Desperation filling his eyes. "Sweetheart, come back to me."

"Daddy?"

"Oh, thank God!" he cried, pulling her close. "I'm so sorry. I should never have fallen asleep—"

She didn't understand. She gazed around. Still at the entrance to the tunnel. The rain had stopped. All was silent.

But then she noticed the tunnel, noticed the red smears along the tracks, the broken refuse littering the rails and the pea stone and—she shivered—were those limbs? Were those hands?

"What happened?"

He pulled away, confusion tugging his eyebrows together. "You…you don't remember?"

She shook her head.

"You were screaming. I was the first one to get up, the first one to reach you before I saw the train. Couldn't even feel the vibration on the tracks with the rain. I couldn't do anything but get us out of the way."

Everyone in that tunnel had died. All because she hadn't woken them up in time. All because she wanted to commune with the rain and the darkness alone. Ella nearly choked. "They're all..."

He pulled her head close to him. "It's not your fault," he was quick to say. "But when I got to you, you were so…" He frowned. "…angry, Ella."

Ella blinked. It was there, smoldering underneath. She wasn't sure why but something had uncaged it, let it loose, fed it… Even the calming waves from her dad's embrace weren't enough to quell it. And that thing that had found her...

She searched left and right for it. Nothing. No eerie shapes. Nothing screaming in agony.

Ella shrunk into her father's arms more. "I'm scared."

"I've got you." He kissed the top of her head. "I always will, Ella."

NINE

Nothingland was an ugly place. Janet had seen plenty of ugly cities in her time. They were all gray or all tan, filled with purposeless billboards, land littered by desiccated factories and outdated shops, lit by old oil drums filled with fire and surrounded by the desperate. But here…

Nothingland was soaked in lights and, almost alcoholically so, in the mock air of mass-produced joy. Joy that came in the skin of erotic dancers at a variety of strip clubs, joy that came in the guise of plastic color-coded chips that could be traded in for any amount of garish, stupid prizes. Joy in the temporary rush of adrenaline provided by a ludicrously fast roller coaster or dangling in a tiny aluminum cage from the top of a Ferris wheel. Joy in violence: any way to make one's own pain belong to someone else.

And joy in the saccharine forgiveness of a religious deity who didn't give a rat's ass what had happened to everyone here on Planet Earth so much as his followers kept believing and praising in Him. Or at least, that's what she expected when she was finally close enough to see this Church that the Junco had spoken about for herself.

The Church is a grotesquely humongous thing standing four stories tall, all Baroque and washed with the shadows of evening, the only light emanating from its red and deep purple stained-glass windows. Full of roses, she thought, though she wasn't quite sure what some of the more unusual shapes in red were meant to be. An audible humming could be heard from inside. The beginnings of Mass. At least, that's what the Junco alluded to.

Janet kept her pace slow, utilizing the shadows as best she could to stay out of sight. While there wasn't so much as a crowd at this time of the night in this part of Nothingland, there were ghosts: people who seemed to appear from anywhere and nowhere and who were immediately forgettable. They all looked the same, she realized. Devoid of a will to live, a will to do anything.

They floated around her and took the front brick walk up to the Church doors before disappearing inside. Her eyes followed the iron fence that lined the road in front of the church, that flared into a rippling gate, chained together in the front. Beyond it lay the graveyard at the western end of the park.

At its gate stood two men in red robes, black crosses swinging from their rosaries. Behind them was a group of men and women gathered around the graves. She wasn't sure why. Perhaps they were paying tribute to someone. That seemed oddly sacred for a place like Nothingland.

Janet remained where she was for a time, wanting to make sure that there weren't any more suspicious shapes lingering in the darkness before she made her move. After all, she still had time before the appointed hour where Mass would begin. Time to make a plan. She needed all of them inside before she could make her move.

She'd been thinking a lot about Hugh as she'd walked from the Garden of Delights to the Church. Thinking about the dad she'd had as a child versus the entirely disparate entity he'd become in her absence. A killer. A man who used his magic to destroy and corrupt and who knew what else. She had always seen him as the more fragile one of her parents, the more emotional one. He was the one who couldn't stand to see her upset even if for the silliest of reasons, the one who always allowed her into their bed whenever she had a nightmare, the one who took the most pictures, and tried to surround her with natural little gifts like beautiful rocks or flowers.

In hindsight, he was also the one who had made sure she knew how to defend herself. He was the one who had sacrificed whatever he had to ensure that she kept going. He was the one who had broken himself for her. And that had made him dangerous. That made him a man with no fucks left to give. A man who had no quarrel with death. A man who wished he could *have* death instead of *be* death.

And she needed him now more than ever.

The corpse of the raven was sprawled beneath a sycamore tree on the edge of the park in front of the Church. The poor creature had been hit with a rock; the offending instrument lay next to it covered in coagulated blood. It's eyes were closed, the side of its skull matted in a tuft of feathers. She could barely see its skull.

Janet bundled the creature into the kangaroo pocket of

her sweater and glanced around the area for what she'd need. She found sticks from an abandoned nest in the tree above, some grass from where it had fallen. There was a half inch of snow that had collected on the curb nearby which she stuffed into her thermos.

All she needed were tears. She'd needed them to bring Amos back the last time.

She'd used spit when she'd tried to bring back Hugh before she knew he was still alive and she'd gotten some decrepit creature barely capable of understanding the most basic direction. She needed to tread carefully.

Janet scanned the park, searching for a safe place where she and the ritual wouldn't be disturbed. Though the tree cover kept the area dark, there was no telling who could come jaunting down one of the many walkways, or blunder across the grass in search of a shortcut. She needed somewhere safer, somewhere—

On the edge of the park directly across from the graveyard was what appeared to be an abandoned food cart, the colorful sign above showing off pictures of soft pretzels. Perfect.

Checking to make sure she wasn't seen, she crept to the pretzel stand and slipped up inside through the unlocked door. Out of the wind and moisture, Janet sat cross-legged on the carpet and went to work.

She pulled her candle from her purse, and planted it before her. After a moment, she tipped her lighter to it to ignite the wick. The flame in the clustered space gave her pause. She'd missed fire. She was used to seeing it as the only source of heat or light in many places and it was strangely absent in Nothingland.

She laid the stiff raven on the rug between her and the candle unscrewed the top of her thermos. She set to breaking up the tiny sticks from the desolate nest, the grass from the park and tossed them into the thermos cup with the snow. Then, she held it over the candle carefully, letting the residual heat melt the snow into icy water.

The bandaged words on her arm were memorized and she spoke them into the darkness: Amos's dedication to Hugh from one of his poetry books. She held the cup of melted snow and roughage over the raven's body and poured out a little offering, watching a few of the sticks topple onto the soft feathers and the moisture roll in rivulets down over its figure. She drank the rest, cautious to chew the sticks and the grass thoroughly before swallowing. It was always awful. She'd never get used to it.

"You told me you'd be waiting for me," she said into the darkness, hoping that Hugh could hear her wherever he was. "Don't keep me waiting too long."

She blew out the candle.

TEN

She was out of time.

The two men in red who had been swapping stories at the entrance to the graveyard were now making their way inside toward the front doors. The people gathered around the grave had filed in through a side door into yellow light only moments before. She wasn't sure how long Mass lasted but guessed it wasn't a quick thing. She'd likely have time to gather a strawberry plant and be on her way back to the Garden of Delights long before anyone inside ever noticed.

Hopefully.

The bells donged high above in the tower, the echo sending a flock of black birds fluttering into the sky from a dead tree beyond the gate. This was her chance. She had to go now.

She couldn't leave the raven behind in as vulnerable a state as it was. She wasn't supposed to move it. The ritual she'd studied had been specific. But if she left it here, locked in this pretzel stand, Hugh wouldn't have a means of getting out on his own. And what if she needed to make a quick exit?

She might not be able to come back and get him…

"Fuck," she murmured to herself as she gently lifted the raven from the floor and placed it in the pocket of her sweater. She packed up the candle in her bag and left the trailer behind to cross the street.

The gates were loosely chained and easy enough for her slight frame to slip under and through the crack between. The wind rustled in the teardrop-shaped Thuja bushes nearby, clicked in the winterberry branches, and whorled against the sharp corners of the church's magnificent façade. It felt empty here and hallowed in spite of the sin she knew lingered. The light struck down upon the snow in painted reds and purples from the stained glass, washing her in its strange patterns as she studied the graves, the ground, ever searching for the wild strawberry.

Inside, a low chorus of voices hummed. The baritone of them made her jaw hurt for some reason, as if they were hitting a particular vibration that made the bones of her body resonate. She wondered what they were doing in there?

Organized religion was never something Amos or Hugh pulled her into, likely because their union wasn't seen as biblically acceptable at the church in the closest town. They told her that nature was their religion and making sure they harmonized with its balance as they accepted its gifts of magic and put whatever they could back into the ground when they could. But there was something about being amongst all those people, the kids in her class, the ones who talked about Jesus and God and feeling secure, knowing that a safe and welcoming afterlife awaited them.

She reached the fence and started along another row

of headstones.

As she'd traveled the country, Janet's understanding of religion was that it was there only to make one feel better about the sins they committed on the daily, be they benign or catastrophic. After all, why would any god, goddess, or deity allow any of this to happen to a world they supposedly cared so much about? To teach us a lesson? If there was one thing Janet knew it was that humans never learned from their mistakes and she was just one of millions exercising that stupid trait.

Janet stopped at the fence and glanced up the next row of headstones. Jesus Fucking Christ. She was going to be here all night if she searched this way. Why hadn't the Junco told her exactly where the wild strawberry plants were supposed to be? The problem with them was that they could be so deep under all the grass so close to the ground that she might not even notice them without some form of unfiltered light. The church windows casting everything in hues of red didn't help her search in the slightest either.

And while she had her lighter and candle, they were specifically for rituals. She worried if she used them for anything other than the purpose she'd been given it for, it would take away from the power of her necromancy spells.

Her vision turned toward the back door to the Church. Perhaps there was a flashlight or some kind of lantern inside she could take? Perhaps they had already harvested some strawberries and she'd find some inside.

Danger.

Red.

Danger.

The idea of setting foot in a church where a Mother Superior character "liked fresh meat" was ludicrous. It was asking for death.

But…

Was she going to light a candle and crawl over every grave in the yard until she found the wild strawberries? She didn't have that kind of time.

Janet absently stroked the bird's feathers in the kangaroo pocket of her sweater and turned back to face the Church.

The Clown's voice arose in her memory. *I'd hate to see you in one of those pits, Janet.*

Me, too, she thought as she climbed up the steps to the back door and crouched by it. She listened. It was hard to hear anything beyond the chorus which had risen in pitch to include loud and impressive arias. There were notes being hit that she could never dream of reaching herself, and imagined the person's head who was singing them turned beet red and swollen with all of the effort.

She couldn't hear any scuffles of footsteps or noises directly on the other side of the door. No voices talking. She thumbed down the old latch and carefully pushed the door in with a soft squeal.

A kitchen: white with pale yellow laminate floors and antique cabinets with carved leaves and grapes swirled into them. An ancient-looking microwave. A pale green fridge that probably pre-dated her by thirty or forty years. Oddly enough, the kitchen smelled empty: no smells of food or anything vaguely edible. Weird.

The voices silenced after another moment and Janet froze in the doorway, unsure if she should keep going or back out.

No, she needed light. She needed to find those strawberries. She let the door shut behind her as she scoured the kitchen for a flashlight. Drawers were slid open as silently as she could make them, several getting stuck from age or warping. There was nothing in the cabinets. Nothing on the counters.

"Tidings!"

Janet's first instinct was to scurry into cover before her brain registered where the voice had come from: a distant room. Before she could stop herself, she crept across the kitchen to the doorway and slinked into the darkened hall.

The voice grew louder. "I beseech you travelers, young and old, to heed the call from Heaven's vast fields. You have sinned. You know you have. God knows you have. But fear not!" The booms become almost soft and pillow-like as they say, "Sanctuary is near if you are strong enough to grasp it."

The hallway eventually opened up into a small cluttered room filled with chairs and cubbies hung with the red smocks she had seen outside on the two men in front of the graveyard gates. Music stands filled with notes stood along the side wall and thick hymnals sat stacked on a table right before a couple of steps leading up to a closed door.

On the other side of it, the great voice continued its sermon. "You have all taken the first step to redemption by answering the Lord's call to worship. Now you must tell Him what you've done and receive his sentence. Can you do it?"

A sickeningly fluent chorus of voices responded, "Yes. We can."

Janet absentmindedly swallowed. *Sentence.* Like a punishment?

"Follow my acolytes and prepare to receive communion and benediction."

Music started up, something clangy and awful and it took her a moment to recognize the discordant shrieks of an organ. She'd once slept in an old Methodist church for the night and her curiosity had gotten the better of her when it came to the apparent piano with dozens of pipes sprouting from it along the wall. The sound had awoken an indignant priest who had thrown her out straight after. That had been a long night.

That same curiosity bit into Janet now. She knew she needed to be concentrating on finding a light. Concentrating on finding the wild strawberries. Concentrating on killing Steele. She knew it yet… The inexorable pull of wanting a peek at the other side of that door was like an itch where she couldn't scratch it.

Ignoring the sourness in her stomach, Janet rested her palm on the doorknob and carefully twisted it, making sure not to make a sound. As the door cracked open, she stared into an enormous nave of the church, the ceilings darting up in theatrical sweeps of buttresses thronged with ornamental curls and dramatic faces, whose hollows seemed to be forever deep. A dome reigned over the room, sectioned like an orange and filled with intricate golden patterns, clouds, and cherubs. Tall windows lined the walls, bursting with fuchsia and vermilion light that cast the room into bloodied shadows.

Janet frowned, mesmerized by the entire spectacle of the architecture until her focus narrowed on the line of parishioners gathered between the pews. The two men in their red smocks stood guard on the steps: one keeping the line at bay while the other brought the next sinner—a young man in a soiled suit shirt and tie—toward a small box at the head of the Sanctuary and sealed him inside.

Mumblings. As much as Janet wanted to hear what they were saying, she didn't want to risk being seen. She scanned the line. There were only twenty or so people: some of whom seemed to be wearing white bandages. She squinted. One over an ear here. Another over a hand there. One taped raggedly to a cheek and stained darkly.

A scream echoed into the heights of the room and Janet's skin burned and froze simultaneously. The sound had come from the box. Moments later, as the door opened and the young man stumbled out cradling his hand, she watched as sheets of blood rippled down over his skin from his fingers…

There was one missing. She had caught a glimpse of it only momentarily but she was sure. She stared at the line of people again. They were cutting off body parts as punishment for sins. Janet gasped and shut the door, barely hearing it click closed as the thundering of blood in her head took over. Fuck the wild strawberries. Fuck the Junco. Janet didn't need her help.

Janet turned and as she did so, she took in the motion of something swinging at her far too late to stop it. Wood clobbered into her head. She plummeted from the steps, her body nothing but a pile of stones. Pain rushed over her like a storm, enveloping her what, her why, and her how.

Gruff hands gripped her arms and a voice breathed down into her face, into the swirls of her hair that covered it. "Broke in, did you? Mother Superior will ensure you're cleansed."

ELEVEN

Her first winter without either of her parents. The caravan had traveled as north as they possibly could, trying to find vestiges of a cooler climate where they might find a water source. They'd settled on a lake, or what was left of it, concealed by ancient pines. There was nothing but an old lifeguard tower there on the beach, an old dock dragged to shore in the off-season and a canoe rack filled with dingy, dented boats.

The community went about their way of setting up their traveling town: the tents went up first, everyone helping secure poles, lay down footprints and tarps, whatever furs and blankets they had for extra insulation. Once everyone had a place to rest, then they erected the canopies and the folding tables and set up what everyone referred to as the Chow Hall.

Ella was only ten but that didn't keep the Taxidermist from putting her to work: hauling furs from her van out to donate to whoever needed them the most. They were heavy and smelled awful in spite of all the care the Taxidermist took to clean and tan them.

She vaguely thought of home, of watching deer in their back field. She'd crouched over the back of the couch next to Amos as they peered through binoculars and counted the spots on the fawns. Remembered the time Hugh had brought her to a farm and she'd petted the rabbits there and fed them kernels of corn. Now, she wore deer skin gloves and a rabbit fur pelt about her shoulders for extra warmth and tried not to think of their skinless bodies.

The Chow Hall united the small cluster in the tail end of the third afternoon hour as the sky was beginning to bruise into violet against a setting sun. With homemade bread and a thick stew filled with whatever meat their resident trapper could supply, vegetables that were often jarred or dehydrated to keep over the winter. It was a feast that first night, the fullest Ella's belly had been in a while and the first time she'd seen something akin to joy on the chapped and beleaguered faces of the people in the caravan. As she'd dipped her fry bread in her stew and ate tiny bites, all she'd thought about were her parents. She imagined them sitting on either side of her, eating, and joking with one another and wondered why, oh why, had they had to leave her?

After dinner, when the lantern lights were soft in the darkness and the wind gusted in across the lake, the Taxidermist and Ella tucked into their sleeping bags, beneath the bear pelt and atop a pillowed fur layers of possums and snowshoe hares to insulate them from the ground.

She cried.

The Taxidermist said to her, "This is how things are now. The loss will never leave you. It's stained in your skin. But if you linger on it and keep dwelling, it'll go deeper. Down into your muscles and your bones. You're just a child. You're too young for that."

She'd blown out the lantern and with an arm to pull Ella toward her, they settled in for what felt like the longest winter Ella had ever felt.

Fingers scraped down into Janet's skull. Her momentary séance with the memory of her first winter as an orphan launched into the back of her mind as awareness took hold. Her hair screamed as someone wrenched her head back, another hand pulling on her arm to get her to her feet. She leapt up to lessen the pain.

"Open the door!" the voice behind her commanded.

Less than a second passed before the fingernails dug into her scalp more. "I said, 'Open it!'"

Janet thumbed down the latch and peeled the door open to the Sanctuary.

The darkness and bloody light from the stained-glass windows welcomed her along with the stares of twenty desperate parishioners. She tried to grab at the hand on her head to loosen its grip but her other arm was pulled up behind her back at an angle that made the muscles sing.

The men in the red robes, one standing at the top of the stairs down to the nave, the other standing beside the confessional, both glanced in her direction, their faces seeming to grow more creases as their brows furrowed. "What've you got there?" the one by the stairs asked.

"Found this little urchin scrambling around in the rehearsal room," her captor hissed. "I thought she'd make a fine amuse bouche for the Mother Superior."

The man on the stairs clapped his hands, a small smile wrapping onto his cheeks. "Splendid! She always gets so tired of the usual communion."

A woman at the head of the line bucked her head. Janet fixed her gaze on the woman's gaunt cheeks and the swaddling of blankets in her arms, a small face there. "But I was supposed to be next!"

"Patience is a virtue," the Man on the Stairs said, shaking his head.

"Everyone here will get their chance to bask in Mother Superior's glow," the man outside the confessional urged. He flicked his fingers toward Janet. "Come. Bring her."

Janet stumbled, trying to trip up whoever was holding her only to feel the pinch of the fingernails, the trickle of something that felt like blood down the side of her head by her ear…

They pushed her toward the small dark box, the man yawning open the door for her to be tossed inside. Janet collapsed over a bench lined with velvet moments before the box door slammed shut behind her.

Spinning, Janet kicked her boots into the door as hard as she could but it didn't budge, something holding it shut on the other side.

In the closet-like space, Janet's head swam. It was dark, the walls close, and the smell like potpourri and mothballs along with…

The stench was unmistakable. The iron-tinged odor was so thick, it made her need to breathe in short gasps. She put a hand to the closest wall and shrunk it back when she felt the slimy glaze of blood on her palm.

"In the name of the Mother, the child, and the holy blood."

Janet's stomach tugged town into her feet. It was the sound of a person who hadn't glimpsed daylight in sometime, someone cast away into the stone bowels of a crypt, kept alive only by the nightmares that others had of it. Janet knew all of these things the moment that it spoke. It wasn't something that should be alive.

And she wasn't sure it actually was.

"Confess to me your sins," it spoke, too close to her in the dark. "Let me consume your ills so that I may pass them on to God."

The lightest touch on her arm, like a moth alighting, made Janet bolt as far back as she could go into the wall. "Don't touch me!" she yelled.

A cough. Choking. No. It was laughter. "How do you expect to be cleansed? How shall God devour all of those horrible deeds?"

Another tugging at her stomach. "Easy; you fucking won't."

Something swept up over her in an instant and Janet's face was suddenly buried in a thick bind of cloth that smelled like sweat and sweet rot. The weight behind it slammed her up against the wall and even as she scrambled and scraped trying to untangle herself from it, she felt panic unleash wildly in her chest.

Swinging blindly, fingers thin as sticks dug into her arms and wrenched them both up over her head while girth the size of which she'd never seen pinned her up against the wall of the confessional.

In the fuzzy darkness, Janet could suddenly see a round thing, with large cheeks veined in purple, lips wreathed by delicate strands of black viscera and eyes that seemed to have no iris, just pupil pinpricked in the center of white. What teeth she could see slathered in dark gore. Unmoving. Unblinking. Like the still image in a horrifying nightmare.

"He wants to taste the darkness you've dreamt," It spoke and craned its head toward her face.

Janet screamed.

And her stomach dropped.

Not her stomach. Her kangaroo pouch. Something in it clambered and flopped and fluttered and burst out, wings flapping discordantly. Black feathers tickled her as she heard the scrapes of talons sinking into the monster's soft white face.

It shrieked, immediately releasing her and throwing itself back against the opposite side of the box. "NO! Nooooo!"

In a sea of dizziness and adrenaline, Janet saw the door to the box crack open and seized the split-second chance to crash into it at full force, knocking the man on the other side over. Outside, the man on the steps was barely holding back a crowd full of screaming, horrified worshipers as they leapt to have their chance in the box. Her original captor, a skeletal-looking old man, made for her, but was stopped short by the huge extended wings of a raven as it swooped down between them, talons burying in his hair.

The door! Janet ran for it, hearing the feverish cries of the crowd behind her as they stomped up the stairs and screamed for the Mother Superior, the cry of an infant lost amongst the clamoring.

She barreled through the door and only caught the shriek of "Janet" moments before the black silhouette bombed through the opening after her. She slammed it, grabbing the closest music stands she could and upending them in front of the door to block it.

"This way!" a familiar voice echoed down the hall in front of her. Janet followed, her boots sliding on the floor, leaving behind streaks of blood on the white tiles. Ping-ponging her body against the doorjamb in the kitchen, she flung herself through the back door to the graveyard and practically collapsed down its steps into the wet grass.

Keep going! She told herself, fumbling along the headstones toward the gates as she squeezed out in between them. The darkness and emptiness of the street met her, refreshed by a small dusting of new snow. It floated down in large flakes all around her as her eyes searched for the darkness of the park. She flung herself into its protective cover.

Amidst the shrubs and low hanging tree branches, Janet kept moving even as the sandstorm of thoughts about what had happened swept down over her. It was only when she'd reached the next block and ducked into an alley that the shakes completely overtook her and she melted down against the nearest brick wall, letting the tears of fright and exhaustion overtake her.

In the distance, the church bells clanged discordantly and screaming filled the night.

She'd almost died. Not just died. Nearly had her face chewed off. But…he'd saved her.

Her dad. Hugh.

As she thought of his name, the bird fluttered down at the head of the alley a few feet away from her, eyes clouded and the bit of his skull still visible, a few feather's ruffled.

The bird took a few wandering steps toward her, beak ajar. "Oh, Jesus." She heard Hugh's voice in her mind as clear as day. "I don't know what the hell you've gotten yourself into, sweetheart, but that—" The bird squawked. "That was an absolutely *horrifying* thing to wake up to."

She scoffed and scrubbed at her wet eyes with the sleeve of her sweater. "Missed you, too, Dad."

TWELVE

Snow collected along the streets and sidewalks of Nothingland as Janet briskly moved down them, letting the distance between her and the Church grow. The raven had perched on the shoulder of her coat for a time but his talons were so sharp and long that they seemed to burrow through the many layers of her jacket and straight into her skin. When she complained, the bird took to the skies for a time.

All the while, Hugh interrogated her, wanting to know all the aspects that had happened between his death and what had happened in the Church.

As the snow picked up and it became nearly impossible for him to navigate in flight, Janet allowed him to nest in the kangaroo pocket of her sweater again and he was sure to keep his claws tucked away from her skin. The pouch swung as she walked.

"And you just *had* to look inside the Church..." Hugh remarked.

Janet huffed. "I was looking for a light."

"Well..." The Raven settled into the material as best it

could. "You cannot go back to the Junco empty-handed. We'll need to find another way to get to Steele without her."

"Weren't you one of his closest bodyguards for, like, seven years?" she asked. "Shouldn't you have some idea of his patterns? What his security is like?"

"His security up until a week ago consisted of me and three other lieutenants but, as we both know, *someone* completely annihilated them and threw a real spanner into his works."

Janet held back an involuntary chuckle. She'd forgotten that her dad called the wrench a 'spanner.' Amos had used to tease him about his British slang for it all the time when Hugh would ask to borrow it.

"As such," Hugh continued, "I have no idea how he's adapted in light of us not being there to cut any of his enemies down. I'd imagine that if people found out we were dead, he'd have had to up his security forthwith."

"Meaning I've made the job harder," Janet grumbled.

"Just because he's got people to shield him doesn't mean they'll have the same batch of skills that we had. We were only four but over seven years, we killed a lot of people for him."

Janet frowned. "You almost sound like you miss it."

The bird shuffled in her pocket and moments later, it's head popped out to stare at her. "I don't. Trust me."

They kept walking until the crosses and religious iconography switched over toward flowers and plants on various shops and over doorways. Janet shivered. She was wet and cold and exhausted. She needed to rest somewhere.

"I can hear your stomach," Hugh muttered.

"Yeah, I haven't eaten since yesterday morning."

"Let me out of here, would you?"

Janet peeled open the kangaroo pocket and after a bit of shuffling, the raven shimmied out and onto the pavement, intermittently walking and hopping as they made their way along.

"How does it feel? Being a bird?" Janet asked.

"Liberating. Suffocating. I'd thought you might bring me back as something more…helpful."

Janet shrugged. "Beggars can't be choosers. There isn't exactly an animal morgue nearby."

"Touche."

They passed a food cart where the vendor was sizzling a combination of onions and peppers on a flattop with oil. Nearby, sausages spun on a rotisserie. Janet's stomach gurgled and a brief thought of trying to steal something bubbled up before her exhaustion crushed it down. Everything hurt. She could worry about food later.

The bird watched her for a moment. In its next hop, it flapped its wings and soared up on an updraft, riding on the current of air from a nearby street vent. Janet watched it take a tight turn and careen back toward the food cart, snatching a prepared sausage roll out of the vendor's hand as he started to give it a customer. Both gasped in surprise and yelled as the Raven tucked into a slow turn and sailed toward Janet.

She held out her hands and the bird delivered it as though it were a boiling hot missile intended for a strike spot. Strips of pepper and onion spilled over onto her fingers and she flinched barely catching the roll itself from escaping out of her grasp. She ran up the concrete to the nearest side street before the vendor and his disappointed customer could lay eyes on her.

The Raven landed on the lid of a dumpster and watched as Janet devoured the sandwich in almost as much time as its delivery to her had taken.

"Easy," Hugh cautioned.

"Fuck you."

"Certainly got a mouth on you in the time we spent apart."

Janet stopped wolfing down the sausage for a moment to glare at him. "I wasn't exactly attending etiquette classes at finishing school." She hesitantly held out a strip of red pepper to him. "Want any?"

The Raven shook its body, its plumage ruffling for a moment before settling into a smooth black swath. "No. Though I'm having a strange craving for worms. Is that typical?"

Janet stared at him, not chewing.

The bird cackled. "Got you."

As soon as Janet was done with her food, and as soon as they made sure the vendor was no longer paying attention, they left the alley, her walking and the bird walk-hopping.

"Did the Junco happen to mention Steele's whereabouts?" Hugh asked.

Janet shook her head moments before a thought occurred to her. "No, but I know where he is."

"Is he in the Tower?"

"No. He's at the Circus. Remember? The one you took me to as a kid?"

Hugh hummed. "I thought he'd lost interest in that. It used to be his place to go to unwind, as it were. I suppose at heart, Steele isn't much different than any other flesh and blood person. He still likes to be amused."

Janet scoffed. Amused by death. Amused by the transience of human life. Amused by other's weaknesses.

"If he's there, that means he's not in the Tower, which is impenetrable. Guards on every floor, security cameras, motion sensors, the works… Even if it were possible for someone to launch a coordinated attack on Steele there, they wouldn't get far. The fact that he's out on the town means he's vulnerable. It means he's not bullet-proof."

"Which means we can kill him," Janet said.

"We can kill him in transit," Hugh specified. "That's when they'll be at their weakest, unsure of where we'll be attacking from and without a solid location to fortify."

"So, we hit him on the way back from the Big Top," Janet answered.

"We can't do it without help."

"But the Junco…" Janet started.

"I have another idea," Hugh answered.

At the end of the next street, the Raven hopped toward the crosswalk and Janet hesitantly followed. "Where are we going?"

"We're going to pay an old friend a visit."

They walked toward north toward the Casinos.

THIRTEEN

She'd left.

As Ella trudged up the hill away from the railroad tracks, she imagined the surprise and possibly annoyance on the Taxidermist's face when she found her ward's sleeping bag, backpack and some of their rations gone earlier that morning. After all, she'd need a head start, something to keep her going until she could find her own supplies.

But for the many years the caravan had taught her about pacing out her provisions to make them last, she'd already run out of water. The train ride had taken her further away than she'd planned, the fear of jumping stymieing her original intentions. The place that awaited her felt as empty as her throat right then: a place dried and bare with nothing but the lattice of hardened mud roads to connect its secluded corners.

Until Janet came across a small warehouse on a road across from what used to be a tiny fire station; nothing but the sounds of cicadas and wood thrushes for miles. Ella ambled closer to it, taking in its buckled white siding, the empty bays where trucks used to back up to it in order to be loaded and the pale rosy light over the door that flickered on in twilight.

But there was something else: a rustling in the woods somewhere far off. Maybe the wind? Janet knew it wasn't. This thing that had followed her all of her life liked to pretend to be the wind. It pretended to be the rain. It pretended to be something ethereal, something beyond touch that had no definite shape most of the time but, if she could catch it just right, she'd see it: the woman with her mouth parted in woe.

It had been years since her encounter with it in the train tunnel, the last time it had been able to get so close to her. But it had watched. She'd sensed its ominous warning in the years that had come and gone since.

For the first time in her life, she had no one there to protect her from it if it decided to come for her.

Fine.

Ella balled her hands into fists and stepped toward the building. Let it try. It wasn't like there was any reason left for her to carry on anyway. She'd do it as long as she could, but honestly? Living with the caravan had grated on her. Watching these people pretend day in and day out that something catastrophic hadn't befallen them, that they were a people committed to living their lives without strife, without blame or grief or fury. Every time they returned to the town she'd grown up in, every time they bartered with the locals as if nothing had happened, she had felt a piece of her placidity chip away.

Where was their offense? Their inner turmoil? Their hatred…?

She couldn't live with people who didn't feel *something*.

As Ella climbed the stairs up to the warehouse and

prepared to open the door, the heaviness engulfed her, pulled at her arms and legs, threatened to drag her down. She knew it was there just over her shoulder: a face warped by anguish, melted in mourning, something that wanted to wrench her down with it to weep in the mire and the mud.

Ella spun around, fire bristling under her skin and in her voice as she screamed, "FUCK YOU!"

Nothing. The air was vacant. The cicadas stopped chirping. The wood thrushes took flight, tiny wings flapping into the wind.

"You'll never get me!" she shouted, her voice lifting into the apricot sky. "So, stop trying and fucking beat it!"

Nothing answered her but the wind.

A light, cool wind.

Ella took a deep and slow breath, allowing the anger to go from its roiling boil to a simmer inside. She didn't think her scream had worked. She didn't think the thing would do what she wanted. But it had heard her, that she was sure of.

And as Ella opened the door to the warehouse and was greeted by the darkness inside, she let the closest thing to a smile lift her face. It was never going to get her. Not if she stoked her ire and let it burn the sadness away.

She'd never let grief touch her again.

FOURTEEN

Casino Town. It sounded like something she'd have seen on television with Amos as they nestled under a blanket together. Hugh wasn't a fan of the old black and white pictures so on the days where he was away practicing music with the orchestra or off performing his piano concertos elsewhere, her father and her would find whatever was playing on AMC and settle in with a bowl of popcorn.

"Casino Town, sugar. Ain't no place like it."

At least, that's what she'd imagined he would have said if he were there with them.

The raven had taken to the sky again, gliding on the air currents as she followed on foot. She was now wishing she was as light as he was, her tire wearing her down. She wished she had some pain relievers or even some caffeine to help lift her out of the exhaustive mire.

"Who are we going to see?" she asked again, hoping Hugh would actually answer her this time.

"I told you: an old friend," he said.

"You do realize that I'm the only one that can hear you, right? You're not going to be able to hug and reminisce on old times when we get there. I have to know what I'm walking into."

"Damn," he muttered. "Suppose I forgot that."

"So?"

"Mark."

Janet blinked. "His name?"

"Yes."

It felt strange hearing someone's name, especially someone she didn't know, but Janet wasn't sure why. After all, everyone still had a name. Maybe it was because she hadn't chosen to learn anyone's name in years. She didn't want that piece of intimacy to tie her memory to them no matter how public the information was.

"And Mark is…"

"He's been holding onto something for me, ever since I saved his life."

"That sounds like a story."

"It does, but we haven't time for it." The Raven landed on a pedestrian walking sign at the next corner. "There." The bird cawed and nodded toward a lit neon sign across the street.

Janet frowned. "Pancake House?"

"They're quite good actually."

She glanced at the other businesses in the area, illuminated by red and green signs for casinos, for hotels and parlors. Even a barber shop that had a slot machine in the window. She turned back to the raven. "This seems very out of place."

"Gambling is an addiction. Even the most serious gamblers still need a place to recharge. Pancake House is one of the most popular eateries here."

"And Mark is the owner?"

"Kind of."

Janet blinked. "Remember what I told you about me needing to know details?"

"All you need to know is that at this time of night, Mark will be sitting at the table in the back corner, drinking a coffee and, likely, will have a stack of pancakes in front of him. Since I won't be able to come inside, this is what you'll need to tell him if we want him to help us."

Janet wrapped her hand around one of the Pancake House's pull bars on the door and it practically floated open under her guidance. The aroma of sweetened batter, of cheap, buttery maple syrup, of bacon wafted around her. It was so strong, it nearly made her sick and at the same time, it made her hollow with longing.

A lone woman at the counter was digging into a stack of pancakes, dripping with a red glaze and decorated with a swirl of whipped cream and Janet's favorite fruit from childhood.

Strawberry pancakes.

Janet's parent's used to make them all the time for her. How had she gone this long and still remembered the smell of them, the sparkle in Amos's eyes as he made them, as sunshine poured in through their kitchen window?

She closed her eyes. *Focus.*

Even in the nighttime, the restaurant was full of patrons slurping coffee and plowing into their breakfast plates like no tomorrow. The olive-green vinyl seats, the wood accents and the brick walls made her feel like she was back at her favorite pizza place in her home town, Secundos. Maybe this is why Hugh used to come here? Why he'd ended up saving this Mark character.

Janet scanned the seats until she found the one in question: a man in his late twenties sat scanning a newspaper on the table. He was thin with a mop of blondish, brown curly hair and a face that Hugh had described in her childhood before as punchable. Young and dumb, maybe the kind of person who always thinks the best of someone which is why they always end up in trouble. Ironically enough, he kind of looked like a younger Hugh.

He sipped from a diner mug full of black coffee and on the table, she noticed a plate full of pancakes, dripping with syrup and a few blueberries dolloped on for garnish. He hadn't taken a bite yet.

Janet walked to the table and stood on the opposite side of it. It took a moment for the man to look up and when he did, he gave a little shake of his head. "What?"

"You Mark?"

He frowned and cast a glance over her shoulder as if he were waiting to see someone familiar pop into view—someone like Hugh. "Who's asking?"

Janet pulled out the chair opposite him and sat before grabbing the fork from his place settings. His half-hearted attempt to stop her ended when she sliced the end of the fork down through his pancake stack, shish-kebobed the pieces on the prongs and slid them off into her mouth.

"It's time," she said between bites.

Mark frowned. "Where's Hugh?"

"Dead."

Mark swallowed. Janet noticed a twinge in his face. They

had been friends after all.

"And he sent me here to get what you're holding for him."

"Jesus fucking Christ," Mark murmured under his breath and put his head into his hands. "This isn't—" As if thinking better, he collected himself and stood up from the table. "Come with me."

Though she didn't want to leave the pancakes behind, Janet got up and followed. Mark rounded the counter, weaving around a waitress coming out with a platter full of eggs and pancakes that made Janet practically drool from the smell they left in their wake. They pushed through the kitchen door into a bustling silver metropolis with men and women slinging food left and right, the steam of several ovens and cast irons cloaking the kitchen in a haze and the smell—five times more powerful and delicious than what she'd encountered in the front of the house.

Mark slalomed through the cooks until he reached a red door in the back of the kitchen that led them down a set of stairs to a small office, the walls concrete and secure. Private.

With the door closed behind them, Janet glanced around at the makeshift office: at the single cot in the corner, the desk with an old-fashioned typewriter set up and books everywhere. On the desk was a framed picture that caught her attention immediately: a black and white photo of Hugh and Amos.

The realization of what this place was hit her at the same time that she noticed Mark holding a bat over his shoulder. "You've got five seconds to tell me—"

Janet turned to look at him and rolled her eyes. "Or what?"

Mark's face twisted in confusion. He looked back and

forth between her and the bat and said, "Well…obviously…"

She used the moment to her advantage, boot kicking up to take out his inside knee. Mark folded onto the floor, his grip on the bat lost as he held his leg. "Shit!"

"I'm not here to kill you. But I don't have time for bullshit." She approached the photo on the desk and picked it up. She'd seen this photo so many times as a child: framed on the bedside table in her parents' room. Amos wearing a gray henley, his large glasses framing his eyes as he laughed, his crooked canine showing mischievously while Hugh held him, his white sweatshirt displaying the logo for his orchestra that he played with. His arm was across his husband's shoulders to pull him close as he planted a kiss on Amos's head.

"Holy shit…" Mark whispered. "It's you, isn't it? You're his…"

She tucked the photo into her pocket. "We're running out of time. Do you have what he left you?"

Mark struggled to get to his feet and limped over to the desk, shuddering open the top left drawer on the desk to pull out…

Keys. More specifically, car keys.

Mark waved her back toward the steps they'd come down and they climbed back up into the kitchen only to veer toward the back exit. In the blustery alley, Mark crossed to a discreet garage door and unlocked the padlock there from a keyring in his own pocket. The door shuttered up to reveal a sight that Janet hadn't seen in what felt like forever.

Her dad's car: a white '88 Pontiac Fiero sat covered in dust and bordered by stacks of cardboard boxes.

"Holy shit," she breathed.

Mark smiled. "Familiar?"

"We had this in my driveway growing up. He had to sell it to get enough money for Amos's medical bills but…" She looked at him. "How is it here?"

"One of the ways I promised to payback your dad when he saved me was by finding this for him. There's not a lot of these still in driving condition around here. It was only a matter of tracking down the VIN number."

"Is that why you gave him the secret room, too? He must have really made an impact on you, huh?"

"Steele had me on a list. Hugh was sent to kill me. But he couldn't. So, he saved my life, got me job here in Casino Town right under Steele's nose, gave a new name…"

Janet exhaled in realization. "Now I get it."

His name wasn't Mark. He was *The Mark*.

"Why stay here in Nothingland when you knew Steele could find you at any minute?"

"Because Hugh wanted him dead just as much as I did. As much as the majority of Nothingland who know what he stands to do. Your dad said the time would come. So, I stayed and ate pancakes." The Mark sniffed and tossed her the keys. "There's a full can of gasoline in the garage. Once you're gone, I'll lock up." He pulled open the door to the kitchen. "And Ella?"

She looked at him.

"Make sure you actually kill that son of a bitch." The door slapped shut behind him.

FIFTEEN

The engine guttered loudly as Janet rode the Pontiac to the end of the alley and rolled down the passenger window. Moments later, the raven flew in, landing in the seat next to her.

"I've wanted to drive her for years but never could," Hugh said wistfully. "I remember thinking about how I'd teach you when the time came. Do you know how?"

"Didn't exactly have a driver's ed instructor but yeah," she said. "The Taxidermist taught me. I sometimes drove the van for her."

"I suppose that's where your fascination for necromancy came as well," he added.

"Maybe." Janet turned the car onto the street and negotiated back in the direction they'd come from.

The heater didn't really work in the old car but that didn't matter so much. It was dry and it cut the winter wind significantly.

"How's the car going to help us take down Steele?" she asked.

The raven pecked at the glove box. "In here."

Janet opened it and frowned. "Is that a block of clay?"

"It's C-4."

She'd heard of that before. An explosive compound. But it needed a detonator.

"In the trunk. I don't keep them together for obvious reasons," Hugh spoke as if knowing what she was going to say.

"So, we're going to blow him up?"

"Yes."

"In transit?"

"That's the plan."

"Which means we need to know exactly where they are going to be and be there waiting before they show up."

The raven turned to her. "Is there something I'm missing?"

"Pre-meditation. The show at the Big Top will likely be ending soon. We need enough time to set the charges and get into hiding where we know we can detonate safely. It's a lot of angles to think about in a short amount of time."

"I didn't think that was your cup of tea, Ella."

She scoffed. "It's not."

"Then you'd better step on that accelerator if you want to give us enough time to prepare," Hugh said.

Janet pressed on the pedal a bit harder.

"Why did you save The Mark?" she asked suddenly. "Why him when you killed countless others?"

"Because he had his family taken away from him just as I did. I've seen it happen dozens of times, but… He had younger sister. She'd have been your age now."

Janet nodded, turning the car at another intersection. "You thought of me."

"Every hour of every day." The raven settled into an ovoid shape on the seat. "I imagined what you'd be doing. What you'd look like. Or if you were already gone."

"I might have been if not for the anger."

The words came slowly from Hugh, as if he wasn't sure exactly what to say. "The what?"

"I stayed angry. Angry about what had happened to me, to you, to Amos. About the injustice of it all. About how nothing was ever going to change. It fed me. It kept me moving. Kept that fucking shadow out of my life until…well. I think the exhaustion has finally caught up with me."

"Stop."

She glanced at the raven. "What?"

The raven hopped to its feet. "I said 'Stop.' STOP!"

Janet pumped the brakes and the car slid to a halt on the frosty road. She stared at him. "What the fuck, Dad? We don't have time for this!"

"The shadow…" His voice seemed apprehensive. "You've seen it recently?"

"It doesn't matter."

"Yes, it does!" The bird fluttered up onto the steering wheel in front of her, black eyes staring into hers. "Where did you see it?"

Uneasily, Janet tried to recollect. "The Carnival. I passed out after getting there from the train."

"Oh, fuck," Hugh muttered, jumping into the seat. "We need to go there now!"

"But what about Steele?"

"Fuck him. Drive!"

Janet stomped on the gas and with the squeal of tires, the car launched forward. She eyed the bird cautiously. "It's just a shadow…isn't it?"

"I should have told you," Hugh lamented as the raven squawked. "I should have told you everything before I left you."

"What? Told me what?"

"It was never just a shadow, Ella. Never just a bad dream. It's a Banshee. And it's been coming for you your whole life."

Janet pushed the accelerator on the car to its maximum, which nearly killed them when she needed to take a sudden right turn. She eased off the pedal but Hugh's words rang in her head, bouncing around inside like a stray bullet. A banshee. What the fuck was a banshee? And why the hell had her parents' lied to her about it?

The road alongside the pits was like a long Slip n' Slide, the snow having built up before the rain. Sleet pelted the windows and the frame of the vehicle as they rocketed through the slush toward the parade of lights on the horizon, toward the shapes of the rotating Ferris Wheel, the bright cotton candy colors of the merry-go-round and the Big Top, the largest tent she'd ever seen which stretched over the lawn.

As they grew closer, it settled on Janet eerily that the light coming from the circus wasn't just from the rides or the arcade or even the string of bulbs that marked the border of the trailers where the circus performers stayed. Fire danced where it shouldn't dance and the air was filled with nothing but its soft roar.

By the time, the car reached the entrance gates, Janet had already flung open her door and threw herself down the empty midway.

Dead. Every unfortunate soul she saw was laid out, bodies studded from bullet holes in the spots where they had performed their last acts. The purveyors of sweet treats lay gutless in the stalls where fried dough blackened to a crisp in the bubbling oil, ride operators crumpled beneath the controls of their great mechanical behemoths, and the clowns…

Janet saw one on stilts that lay like a discarded doll between two tents: one that sold cheap rings and the other with a fortune teller who lay face down on her table. She rushed to the clown and her heart soared when she realized it wasn't him. It wasn't The Clown.

"Ella!" Hugh shouted after her, the raven soaring above.

She ran on, taking in more dead bodies, more rides still spinning and gyrating without attendees to ride them, more of the carnival freaks plugged in the face or the throat or several times through the chest.

This was because of her. She knew this. Steele had somehow found out where she came immediately after she got off the train and he'd decided to make her pay for ever coming here.

Music played from the Big Top tent and Janet somehow knew that was where she would find him. Pushing through the entrance flap, she ran down the corridor between the metal bleachers until the center ring opened up beneath the cold floodlights from above. Lying propped up against one of the platforms was The Clown, holding his stomach, a trail of blood skimming his lips down to his chin and further still down his neck.

Janet ran to him and pressed her hand to his clammy one. "That fucker… That fucking fucker…" she rumbled.

The Clown took a shaking breath. "Jan…et?"

"I know it's going to hurt but you've got to get up, okay?"

She tried to wrap her arm around him and hoist him up but her own body withered beneath his weight and they both crashed back down.

The Clown squeezed her hand in his, his breaths turning to wheezes.

She reached out and put her hand to his head, to his brow, her thumb pushing through the sweep of sweat-laden hair there. "What's your name?" she asked him.

"K-Klaus."

"Steele's as good as dead," she started. "I'll make sure—"

The Clown's head settled as he stared at a spot over her shoulder and with a rattle in his exhale, he stopped moving all together. Janet opened Klaus's hand tangled in hers to reveal a skeleton key.

Janet knelt there, head hung. She wanted to cry. She wanted to feel *something* deeper than hatred, something human, something that would make her remember that she wasn't just a thing that death followed around after, killing in its wake. But it didn't come. Tears didn't come.

All that did was the desire for absolution: a ball of flame twisting in her gut.

She left the Big Top.

The raven waited for her, perched on the corner of a stand selling funnel cakes. "Ella…"

"It's fucking Janet now," she grumbled, walking in the direction of the trailers. "How many fucking times to I have to tell you people?"

"You can call yourself something different but you're still my—"

"Your what?" She spun toward him. "Your precious

innocent daughter? You lied to me, Hugh. You and Amos. This fucking shadow has done more than stalk me. It's killed coming after me. And now you're going to fucking tell me why."

"It's complicated. Would you…" The raven swooped overhead and landed on a gate to a ride a little further down. "Could you just wait?"

"There's no time."

"We don't know where Steele has gone. We don't have a plan. We need to wait and think things through!"

"I'm done with waiting."

The sleet tinkled like grains of salt against the metal trailers across from the midway. Janet quickly located the Clown's trailer and, by extension, the caged animal in the back of it.

The lion paced in its cage, growling. Janet could feel its agitation. As she closed in on the lock, the raven dove in from above closing its claws around the key and flapping its wings. "No! What the fuck do you think you're doing?" Hugh yelled.

"It's not going to kill me," Janet screamed back, yanking the key from its grip.

The bird awkwardly fell to the ground, fluttering to get back to its feet. "Ella, don't!"

She clicked the key into the lock and turned it.

The lion paced toward her as the door opened, its massive paws braced. Before she could stop it, the lion rushed past her, shoving her aside as if she were nothing more than the breeze. She collapsed on the ground beside the raven as the lion sprinted for the midway.

"You're mad!" Shock tinged Hugh's voice. "That's a fucking *lion*. It'll hunt down and kill everyone it can and—"

Janet got to her feet and turned away from him, moving to the door for the Clown's trailer and climbing inside. The heater blasted warm air into her face as she tucked up inside, letting the door shut behind her. Moments later, a steady pecking ensued on the other side. Sighing, Janet let the raven in.

It flapped up into the small space, landing on the kitchen counter top. "Blimey, it's hot in here."

Janet collapsed on the Clown's bed against the soft covers for a moment. "I'm tired of watching people die. Good people. People who try to be kind," she said. "Do you know how exhausting it is?"

The bird studied her. "I do."

"I need you to tell me about the Banshee, Hugh. This time, don't think you're protecting me by keeping anything to yourself. I'm not a child anymore. Unless you want me to die, you'll give me all the facts. Right now."

"Alright." The bird croaked. "I'll tell you."

SIXTEEN

"A Banshee," Hugh began, his voice tremulous. "I'd always heard of them as a boy. Creatures of myth: usually Irish in origin though there are many other cultures that embrace the narrative of the wailing woman. But that's all they were to me: stories.

"When I met your father, we both had individual dreams about having a child. About caring for one, that is. After years passed and we finally got round to talking about it, we decided that we should find a surrogate. After all, we wanted you to be as close to us as possible. We wanted you to share in our magic gift. We found someone willing to act in that role for you and I…well…donated, so to speak."

"I get it," Janet interrupted. "You fucked a woman for the sake of having a baby."

"Yes, well, if we're whittling the act down to its most primal description…"

"What happened next?"

"About mid-term, we received a call that your birth mother had been involved in some sort of altercation. When we checked in on her, she told us she was being haunted. She said they were ghosts, shadows that existed in her periphery that loomed closer and closer when she couldn't focus on them. And while we practiced our own version of magic, your father and I had no reason to suspect that anything supernatural might have been happening. We really thought she was disturbed.

"As the months continued, her visions got worse. Up until the day of your birth that is. It was her clearest day in months she'd said. Shortly after you were born, however, your birth mother vanished. No one remembers her leaving the hospital, no one saw her return to her home and pack. It's as if she were carried away on the wind by a scream."

Janet stared at the bird, trying to piece together the information thus far. "And that means…?"

"We didn't notice anything was wrong until the first time you screamed in your sleep," Hugh answered. "It was a lonely scream. A keening you could call it. Like one of them, I imagine. And then, they started actually showing up: physical manifestations for us to contend with as your visions worsened."

"What's so scary about them?" Janet cocked her head. "They're nothing but crying ladies. The world has its fair share of them."

"They're not just crying ladies, Ella. Wherever they go, they bring with them an omen. They are the harbingers of death and decay. A couple years after yours started showing up is when Amos…" Hugh's voice died.

Janet flew up from the bed, her cheeks tingling. "What? Are you saying *I* did that to Amos? That I…"

"Ella, I never meant to suggest—"

"You just did," she snapped. "You *suggested*."

"I suggested that the Banshee heralds death. Nothing more." Hugh's voice cracked. All the raven did was blink. "I don't know how it knows where death is going to be. I don't know why it latched itself onto you. But I know that it has. And whenever it shows up…wherever… Something bad happens. People die."

Janet thought about the instances when the shadow had shown up in her life. Before Amos started to lose his memory, all the people who hadn't survived in the tunnel when the train came barreling through, many times over her years skirting Out There when death had touched her pursuers or enemies. Even when she had arrived at the hotel to take on all of Steele's body guards, she'd felt ghosts. A presence.

"If this thing wanted me so bad, why didn't it ever take me?" Janet asked.

"That anger you have, what's been keeping the Banshee at bay…" He sighed. "That was Amos's fault."

The way he said felt like a toss over his shoulder type of comment, one that made Janet immediately bristle. "What do you mean 'his fault?'"

"That last time we went to see him before he—"

"I remember."

"When he touched you, he imbued you with a protection spell, one that I tried time and again to lift but couldn't. Anger. He felt that it was the only thing that could keep you alive, the only thing that could buoy you from the woe and the fear that creature projected."

Janet regarded her hands. Her father, even in his delusional state, had known she was in danger. But why anger? Why not joy? Why couldn't he have given her something positive that could seep into her blood…

Because it wasn't dangerous enough. She knew the answer immediately. Rage flared hot and fiery and while it burned up quickly like a paper filter, it was more powerful than any amount of joy she'd be able to cobble together in this existence, she was sure of that.

Janet started for the door.

"Where are you going?" Hugh asked.

"To end this once and for all." She turned the knob.

The raven uttered a sound that sounded so much like a sob that it made the hairs on Janet's arms rise. "I'm sorry. I'm so sorry, El—Janet. I was lost without your father. I thought I could do it on my own. I never wanted any of this for you."

She thought of Hugh crying himself to sleep night after night, how choked up he was to the point that he couldn't even say Amos's name in the hotel… The photo she'd found in that secret room in the Pancake House… Yes. He had made bad decisions. He had kept things from her. But his intentions had been with love even if he had broken her heart.

Janet allowed a steady inhale to fill her before pushing it back out through her nose. She nudged her head toward the door. "Come on."

The raven jumped from the counter to her waiting shoulder, his grip loose enough so as not to catch her with his talons but steady. "Steele has probably already returned to the Tower at this point. There'll be no getting to him now."

"Steele will get what's coming to him soon enough but he's not my priority right now," Janet said.

"Wha… What do you mean?"

"He only knew that I came here to the Carnival because someone told him I did. And aside from you, that leaves only one person."

The bird crouched on her shoulder, its head low and eyes quizzical. "Who?" Hugh asked.

"Your fellow feathered friend," Janet said, her tone darkening. "The Junco."

SEVENTEEN

One wrong move was all it would take which is why they had to act as fast as possible. It meant not letting the Junco see them coming. It meant the element of surprise.

When the Garden of Delights came into view through the windshield, Janet asked Hugh if he was ready. The bird merely fluttered in the seat next to her and squawked. She stepped harder on the accelerator, one hand braced on the steering wheel and the other holding onto the chest strap of her seat belt as she veered the car off the road and toward the glass front doors of the Garden.

"Oh fuck," Hugh murmured as the car slammed into the glass entranceway.

Janet's body snapped forward, the seatbelt barely keeping her in place, her feet crashing into the pedals while her knees jammed into the dash beneath the steering wheel. Glass shattered, raining down over the car in a sheet of rippled shards painted with the pink glow of the grow lights. The metal framing of the doors cascaded across the lobby, hanging plants yanked down and pots tipped this way and that.

Before the torrent of their entry had fully taken effect,

Janet had already unbuckled her belt, trying to catch her breath and rubbing at the soon to be bruise from left shoulder to right hip. Somehow, the car door still opened, creaking as it let her into the massacred space. Catching herself on a table full of magazines in the destroyed waiting area, she stumbled forward, trying to get her balance under control as she approached the plant garden and the pool, still filled with lounging addicts. No one had reacted to her entrance.

Behind her, Hugh's strained voice called to her. "Suppose the car was going to end up like this eventually."

"That's pessimistic," she answered under her breath, steadying herself on the edge of the fountain.

"What makes you so sure the Junco gave you up?" he asked.

"She asked me where I got my coat because she recognized it. The Clown knew who the Junco was right away which means he probably visited here. She'd seen him in it before. She knew I had come from there and that someone had helped me."

The raven waggled its head. "When we did business together, she kept my secrets for me as I kept hers. Why would she betray that trust we fostered?"

"Easy." Janet stood and moved to the other side of the lobby, back toward where she knew the secret elevator lay. "Because she didn't have faith in me that I could get the job done. I'm used to people underestimating me. Always makes getting even that much sweeter."

"Or she was afraid," Hugh inferred. "Going against Steele is a dangerous game. If she thought you weren't capable of it and knew that I was dead, she'd have to feel as though the safer route was in denying she had ever planned on mutiny against him.”

“Fear makes people do stupid things, or in this case, it makes you double-cross your friends to save your own neck.” Janet prodded at the wall, searching for the curtain. God, it was dark back there. Where had that Guide been when she pulled back the curtain? A moment later, her fingers dropped on the silky satin of the curtain and she pulled it aside to reveal the matte black doors. She punched the button and waited until the doors sliced open to that sleek red interior.

The raven blinked. “She changed the color. Bold choice.”

Janet stepped inside and the raven swooped in to alight on her shoulder as the doors closed. She selected the top floor and the elevator rumbled to life.

“She’ll have felt that impact, if not heard it. Locked herself in that office,” Hugh said. “How do you expect to get her to come out?”

“By lying through my teeth.” She glanced at the bird out of the corner of her eye. “Just be ready to do your thing when the moment presents itself.”

The bird let out a throaty ruck sound.

With a soft ding, the doors parted and Janet threw herself down the hallway at the fullest burst of speed she could. When she reached the door at the end, she banged her fists on it. “Open up! Junco!”

On the other side, a scuffling sound of someone moving around reached her, heels on a hardwood floor for a moment before being deafened by a carpet. Then, lowly, from the opposite side of the door. “Janet?”

“I’ve got the wild strawberry!” she proclaimed, adding as much tremulous, simulated fear into her voice as she could.

"They're coming for me! Followed me back here! Open up!"

Above her, she heard the swish of wings in the air, the slight flap and barely saw the iridescence of the raven's feathers before they vanished into shadow.

The door unlocked and after a moment opened.

Janet pushed herself inside, making sure to drive her shoulder forward.

The Junco, on the other side of the door, teetered off balance from the sudden shove, arms flailing to keep her feet planted.

The raven dove inside, wings pulled back until it could angle itself back into the air and flap them once to stop and pivot. The creature then divebombed toward the Junco's hand with the gun in it and snatched it from her.

Well, almost.

The raven didn't so much as grab it as it did knock the weapon from her hands. It clunked across the ground, sliding with a swirl at Janet's feet where she immediately picked it up and turned its muzzle on its owner.

The Junco waved her hands in the air wildly searching for the winged demon that had attacked her before she fully recognized her predicament. Her eyes bulged into shock. "Janet, what do you think you're doing?"

"You sent me into that Church to die," she said definitively. "I didn't."

The raven landed on the corner of a bookcase nearby and cawed.

The Junco's shock glazed over into fascination. "It *is* you. I heard stories about a young woman killing Steele's lieutenants. Had a wild animal companion with her: a fox, I think. I figured someone was lying somewhere along the way, like the game of telephone where the story gets blown out of proportion every time it gets passed along? But they weren't lying, were they?"

"How about we get back to the part where you sent me off to die because you didn't think I could manage to kill Steele?" Janet thumbed back the hammer on the gun. "How about now?"

The Junco put her hands up on either side of her head. "I was wrong. I should have trusted you. If Hugh did, then I should have. I won't make that mistake again."

"You won't, will you?" Janet brought the muzzle of the gun closer to her face. "Any other mistakes you ought to learn from? Oh, how about the fact that you snitched on me to Steele about the Carnival. So, he went out there and murdered them all."

Janet noticed a sizeable lump grow in the Junco's throat at the words. "I…I didn't think he would—"

"Bullshit," Janet rumbled. "You went on about the four corners of Nothingland and how its leaders don't step into each other's category. I'll bet you negotiated your own little piece of the land the carnival sits on for yourself, didn't you? Every motive you've had so far has been an entrepreneurial linchpin for your Garden Empire in Nothingland."

The Junco shuddered before collecting her dropped cigarette in its long holder from the rug nearby and giving it a long pull. Smoke oozed from between her lips as she said, "This business is all I've got left. Some people would kill to keep their family's safe. This is my home; the plants are my loved ones. Even those pathetic losers down there draped all over the florals are like my children. I'd do anything to make sure I don't lose it."

"Then give me what you have on Steele," Janet said. "I won't kill unless I have to. And I'd much rather see Steele in the ground than a woman trying to make whatever kind of living that she can for herself. You understand? I didn't come here for you. I came here to finish the business I have with him."

The Junco nodded. They were small at first but as the moments passed, the nodding grew bigger until a feverish smile crept across her lips. "We ladies have to stick together, don't we?"

"So…" Janet cleared her throat. "What intel do you have?"

The Junco took another drag from her cigarette, her dark eyes dazzling. "Most people think that Steele hides up at the top of his Tower every minute of every day. The speculation is that he hates to mingle with the rest of the poor bastards down below, or that he's too afraid that someone might see him for who he is and kill him. But Steele isn't afraid and while he speaks as though he's superior to the mindless fucks who inhabit this place, he can't help but relish in their behavior either. After all, what was Peter Pan but a Lost Boy himself, wasn't he? He simply can't help himself."

"So, he tries to blend in every once in a while?" Janet asked.

"He picks different days of the week, goes to different spots around Nothingland to, as he calls it, 'have a gas.'"

Janet glanced at the raven, but Hugh remained silent. She looked back at the Junco. "And tonight?"

The Junco's smile turned devilish. "Let's just say he likes to catch a show every now and again."

Backing up across the room to the map on the wall, Janet gripped it by the corner and pulled it down, a few tacks falling as she crossed back over to the Junco and laid it down at her feet. "Where?"

The Junco pulled the cigarette from her mouth between her thumb and forefinger and tipped the end toward a location in the southwest, leaving a singing spot amidst the town of Nothingland.

"Thanks," Janet said and pulled the trigger.

The geyser of blood and brain matter smacked the floor and door and part of the nearest wall and, somehow, none of Janet.

"Not exactly what you promised," Hugh remarked, the bird's gaze discerning.

"She killed a whole circus," Janet growled. "She was fucking evil."

"Her intel is bollocks," Hugh added. "Steele goes out on these little jaunts but he always brings back up with him, enough men to constitute a small army and all of them hide decently out of sight."

"Guess it's a good thing that we have your C-4 then," Janet said, a smug smile painting her face. "We wouldn't want to have to get up close and personal."

EIGHTEEN

"Fuck."

Janet wanted to punch the car. Punch a plant. Punch one of the high customers who hadn't moved once since she'd launched and succeeded at her attack on the Garden of Delights. Hell, maybe even punch Hugh for having a pathetically old car that had been more adorable than practical. It wouldn't start, no matter how much she wrenched the key to try and turn over the engine. Worse: she'd broken the glovebox in the crash and it wouldn't open.

"There's got to be a prybar around here somewhere," she said more to herself than her bird companion. "Something I can use as leverage to wrench this thing open."

"Unless you're going to find a super strong, sentient plant to do the trick for you, I don't think it's going to happen," Hugh said. "Why couldn't you have pulled up on the street corner and jumped out like any normal person?"

Janet crouched down and tossed debris from the destroyed doorway aside, searching for something useful. "Because she had to believe my coming here was life or death. She had to believe that I still thought she was innocent and she had to be pissed enough at me to make her think that killing me was her only option."

"Well…" The raven flapped its wings a couple times. "I think we're what your father would call 'up shit creek.'"

She cracked a smile, a smile that turned sour in the seconds that passed. "I miss him."

"Me too," Hugh said solemnly. "Whenever I was in a mess and didn't know what to do, Amos helped me sort it out."

The two of them remained there for a moment. If only she could bring him back too… Janet knew there wasn't time to track down a dead animal to perform a ritual on. Even if she could find one, it would take hours for Amos to reanimate and that was time they didn't have.

She stood and picked up the Junco's gun from where she'd left it on the driver's seat of the car. "Let's go."

The raven crooked its head in her direction. "Do we have a plan?"

"No. But that hasn't stopped me before."

She climbed over the rubble from the destroyed entrance, stone and glass crunching under her boots as she finally made it back out to the street. The raven soared out and up to perch on a stop sign.

"Now," she said. "Which way is it to the theater?"

The bird took a moment to orient itself and once it had, flew off.

Janet gave chase.

The theater was a spectacle: a brick façade offering windows kindled by an amber light and red awnings, a ticket box and shining stanchions over a velvety green carpet to guide whoever wished to see a show inside. And it was eerily quiet.

For most of Janet's time in Nothingland, she'd been surprised at how normal of a city it had felt. When the Clown had told her about it, she'd expected mayhem at every turn. She'd expected people to be smashing into windows, setting fires, screaming and engaging in general chaos. After all, that's what it was like in a number of different places still: why not in Steele's convenient little attempt at Pleasure Island?

But it wasn't like that at all. It was so…normal seeming, despite what purportedly happened behind closed doors. When she asked Hugh about it, he cavalierly answered, "As it turns out, the thing that most people desire is for things to be the way they were. All of their micro-fantasies and horrible perversions can be met in private and they can go out for a coffee afterward. The world still feels like its turning."

Janet kept the gun concealed in her coat pocket wanting as much of an element of surprise as she could have for when she came face to face with Steele. And shortly after she reached the front doors, she stopped. She realized she had no idea what Steele even looked like.

"How do I know which guy in here is Steele?" she asked.

"I'll tell you. Don't worry," Hugh assured.

Janet stepped through the doors and froze. The entire foyer was in a state of utter disarray. Popcorn lay strewn about the floor along with various cups and buckets while several stanchions and velvet ropes were yanked down and tangled. Programs had fluttered all over the floor and there was absolutely no one in sight.

Distantly, Janet thought she heard a scream.

"What the hell happened here?" Hugh said before she could.

Her hand firmly on the still-concealed weapon, Janet climbed the steps up to the concession stands and peered behind the counter for some kind of clue. No one there either. But…she blinked. Reece's Pieces. She yanked a box from behind the glass case, busted into it and dumped a handful in her mouth.

She was transported. A child laughing with Amos and Hugh as they took her trick or treating through town on Halloween, dressed like characters from *the Wizard of Oz*. They'd bought her a wig with pigtails and a small dress so she could be Dorothy, but she'd wanted to be the lion instead. So, Hugh threw on the wig and found a blue pleated shirt at a discount store. With Amos dressed up like the scarecrow, they were the perfect ensemble.

The raven fluttered in and landed on the counter in front of her. "As much as I enjoy seeing you smile, we don't have time for that right now."

Janet stuffed the box into her other pocket and resumed the search, all memories doused once more in her focus to find Steele. To the left and right behind the concession stands were the doors to the theater and as they got closer, the intermittent screams grew louder. With her back to the nearest wall, Janet snuck up on the doors and peered inside.

The room was impressively decorated, the wallpaper full of golden fleur-de-lis against an emerald backdrop with rows and rows of stall seats leading down toward the stage and the projector screen that encapsulated the entire space. The seats were speckled with attendees who cowered, emitting horrified whimpering and all staring at a muscular creature as it gorged on a body in the front row.

The lion.

The Clown's lion had made it here on its own.

"What did I tell you?" Hugh murmured. "What did I say? I knew it was a terrible idea to let that thing out."

Janet smirked. "Not if it's eating the assholes who killed its owner."

The body lain out underneath the animal was clothed entirely in black and a discarded weapon nearby told her it had likely been one of Steele's bodyguards. *So,* Janet thought, *where is that fucker hiding?*

"J-Janet!"

She pinned herself to the wall, caught off guard, not by the fact that it had known her name, but by the voice…

No… It can't be.

Janet peered back into the theater, searching high and low and high—until she saw him. Until she saw the small, fuzzy shape perched on the lip of one of the theater boxes above. A marten. *The* marten that she had last seen running away from her on the Man's front lawn.

She dropped to her knees. "Amos?" she croaked.

The raven fluttered. "Amos!" Hugh cried.

But he had died? She had heard the animal's terrible scream that night as the dogs chased him down.

With renewed determination, Janet slid into the room and took cover behind the rear row of chairs, her eyes locked on the animal above.

The raven bombed into the room, cruising straight for the marten. "Amos!" Hugh yelled again and Janet could feel the pain in it almost like being burned.

But if Amos was here in the marten's form, it meant that someone had captured him that night in town. It meant…

"Don't!" she yelled at Hugh seconds before the raven's body reached the balcony and landed next to the marten. Seconds before a hand appeared with something gleaming in its grip and hit the bird with enough force that Janet heard the thunk from across the room. Jolted she watched as the raven plummeted down, hitting the edge of the stage before it landed on the rug.

NINETEEN

"**N**o!" she screamed, digging for the gun in her coat but finding the Reese's Pieces instead. Tears blinded her as she flung the box aside and searched the other pocket until she came up with the gun.

Amos wailed Hugh's name from above.

The lion, spooked by the noise, snarled and leapt up, padding toward the far side of the room. The people hiding in the chairs there shrieked.

"So," a cautious voice called down from the balcony. "We finally meet."

Janet gnashed her teeth. She didn't know if Hugh was dead. All she knew was that Amos was in danger and that fucker, Steele, was up there in the balcony out of the lion's reach.

For now.

As she studied the room, she noted the staircases to the balcony on opposite sides of the stage. All she needed to do was lure the cat up there.

"Oh, I didn't think that you were the kind of person to give the silent treatment," Steele called. "Where is that vexation you showed when you came for that blubbering old fool in town that night? Or when you slaughtered my generals in the hotel? You're a crafty bitch, Janet…or should I say, Ella."

"I'll take that as a compliment, you slimy fuck," she returned.

Steele laughed. "You weren't expecting to see your little pet, were you?"

Amos cried out and Janet glanced out from cover to see that the marten was now gone from the platform.

"Vicious little thing," Steele commented. "Took a shock collar to finally train it."

Heat radiated off of Janet's skin as her rage built. She needed to kill him. She needed to get her hands around his—

"Focus," she heard Hugh say weakly in her head.

He was still alive! But she didn't know for how much longer…

Janet fought around the emotion, thoughts clambering with what she needed to do. If she could get down to the front of the room, lure the lion up the stairs to the balcony, then she could let it loose on Steele. She didn't think he had a gun, but she wasn't sure if any of his other cronies were around. Hugh had said he'd have multiple bodyguards…

The shuffle behind her caught her attention moments before she turned and saw the pistol aimed at her. Janet ducked and rolled, the gun firing, bullet striking the seat nearest to where she'd just been. Her own wasn't even out of her pocket before she fired, her coat pocket bursting at the same time that the bodyguard's throat bloomed open. He struck the ground in front of her.

How the hell had he snuck up on her? Janet whirled to make sure there were no other attackers and pivoted when she saw a set of stairs she had missed in the lobby outside the entrance to the theater, switchback stairs that ascended to the balcony floor. Stairs that, at that very moment, another crony of Steele's was clambering down, gun in hand. She rose the Junco's gun and fired as he reached the mid-landing, but missed, the bullet striking the newel post instead.

The bodyguard ducked back behind the cover of the top flight of stairs.

She took aim with the gun again, waiting for him to poke his head back out and when she did, pulled the trigger.

Click.

Janet stared at it, popping open the cylinder to find it empty. She hadn't checked it to even make sure it was full. How stupid was that? And how stupid that the Junco only left it with two bullets loaded.

She tossed the gun. She searched the thug who had dropped in front of her but couldn't find his gun. Maybe it had fallen under the seats? She couldn't go belly down to search or she'd be as good as dead.

A realization: there was a weapon down at the end of the theater near the massacred body of the lion's victim. She heard the henchmen's heavy footfalls thumping down the stairs as she leapt out of cover and ran for the stage front, her eyes locking on the lion that had sequestered itself on the opposite side of the stage, pre-occupied at swatting at a couple who had somehow managed to climb up toward the lowest theater box.

Zeroing her sights on the gun, Janet threw herself down onto the ground to retrieve it and rolled to meet the bodyguard. She put two bullets in his chest. The lug collapsed in a heap in front of her.

In all the commotion, Janet wasn't sure if Steele was still up in his private theater box, wasn't sure what he'd done to Amos, but she knew she'd need to act fast. Even as the thoughts collided, her sights settled on the raven lying on the floor now only a few feet from her. She scuttled over to it and lifted it into her arms. "Hugh…"

"Things are broken," he sputtered. "It's no matter. I'm a ghost in a dead thing anyway. Concentrate on Steele."

Over her shoulder, Janet heard a bristling huff and a micro turn of her head confirmed that the lion's attention was now focused on her as it loped from the other side of the stage.

Laying the bird down on the stage next to her, Janet ran, her feet pushing her up the nearby staircase to the balcony. Her head pounded with the rush of adrenaline, with the hot pulse of resurging anger. Oblivion stabbed at her heels as the creature behind her bounded up the steps.

She couldn't outrun this thing. She only had one chance at this if it was going to work.

The hall to the balcony and the subsequent theater boxes stretched before her in the dim lights. She pushed her legs with everything she had, her breath ragged. She reached the curtains for the box: the one she'd last seen Steele in and threw open them open.

And there he was.

Janet had had all kinds of mental pictures of what Steele would look like. Sometimes, he was blond. Sometimes, he was a brunet. Sometimes, he had a sleek mustache like cartoons she'd seen of dastardly villains. In all of them, his face was chiseled and eyes blue with the grizzled stubble that all leading Hollywood actors had had when she was growing up: people like Chris Pratt and Henry Cavill and Ryan Reynolds…

He was older than she had expected. The movie-star charm of his glory days reduced by middle aged wrinkles and silver strands that overtook his blonde ones but she had been somehow eerily right about his blue eyes, how they dissected, even with the one furious and confused glance that he threw in her direction as she blundered into the box.

The scruff of the marten was tight in his right hand as he held out the wriggling animal over the edge of the balcony. In the other was a silver cane with a sharp point at its end. She'd not been able to tell what had hit the raven before. Steele brandished it to strike her if she got any closer.

He was going to either stab her with the cane or drop Amos or both. And if she didn't rush him, the lion would do worse things, she was assured.

The tearing of claws on the rug at the end of the hall made her decision for her and she burst forward into the box.

Steele pulled the cane back to stab it at her, an action that she narrowly avoided by vaulting over the back of the seats next to him. One moment, he was holding Amos, the next his hand was empty. Janet felt the fear punch her in the gut moments before his now free hand did the same.

Crumpling to the floor, she only had a moment to roll onto her side before Steele's shoe stomped on her free hand. Bones crunched and Janet screamed.

"You think you can take this away from me," he snarled, poking the pointed tip of the cane at the hollow in Janet's throat. "You think some little sad brat like you can—"

He didn't get to finish his sentence before a locomotive of fur and muscle slammed into him, breaking his back against the balcony's edge before they slid down onto the floor beside her. Steele's screams resounded through the open acoustics of the theater along with the lion's snarls as it dug her jowls into his neck and face.

Letting the heat of the moment distract the cat, Janet picked herself up off the ground and carefully sneaked back out into the hallway, making sure to slide the curtains closed behind her. Noxious crunching faded into the background as she hobbled to the stairs and descended.

Amos.

Panic bucked in her chest as she rounded the landing and covered the last flight before stumbling out onto the first floor of the room. She scanned the rug for the bird and the marten but found neither. "Hugh!" she called. "Amos!"

She heard Amos's soft voice moments later coming from further up the aisle. The marten was crouched over the raven, which lie like a discarded toy on the carpet. When Janet knelt down next to them, Amos said, "He saved me. Somehow got up enough strength to catch me before we crash landed."

She reached over and picked up the raven gently. "Hugh?"

The raven blinked its milky eyes at her. "Did we…"

"It's done."

She heard him sigh. "Amos?"

"I'm here." The Marten clambered into Janet's lap, placing its paws on her arm to see him better.

"I'm so sorry," Hugh murmured. "About everything. About leaving you…"

Amos shushed him. "I know you did everything you

could do."

As her parents talked, Janet scooped them both into her arms and carried them out of the theater. The rest of the frightened attendees had fled once the lion made its way upstairs and it was now just them and the music from the lobby as it played an old ragtime tune over the speakers. Janet rounded the concession counter and knelt on the floor there with the animals to survey their bodies.

Both looked rough. The raven's wings were mangled, delicate bones poking out from the torn feathers and flesh while its beak hung open. She knew this body had had it: Hugh had had it.

The marten's body had deteriorated in the months Amos had inhabited it as well. She recognized scars all across it from various things: burns, scratches… The anger in her sizzled. Steele had done that to him because he'd known he was special to her, even if he hadn't known the real reason why. But the worst wounds were the ones just inflicted, the punctures from the raven's claws when it had tried to save the marten from the fall…

She knew what needed to be done. Her heart swelled and she violently pushed back the acceptance and the anguish she knew would follow. *Stay hot. Stay angry,* she told herself, her fists balling.

Amos set a paw on her knuckles. "It's over, sweetheart," he said. "There's no need to feed the flames anymore."

And try as she might, she just couldn't extinguish them this time. Her eyes flooded as she said, "But I just got you both back. It's not fair…"

"You know very well that life is almost never fair, darling,"

Hugh said, his voice faint. "This life has taken so much from you and you've held yourself together against its storm. But it's time for you to settle now. It's time for you to have peace."

Janet swallowed, trying to talk through the tightness of it. "I can't without you both. We lost all of our time together."

"And someday," Amos chimed in, as the marten curled into a ball next to the raven. "We will be together once again. But you can't keep holding onto ghosts. And… I'm so tired."

"Please, darling," Hugh said. "Start fresh. Anyone can begin again. Even you."

Janet sniffed, tears dripping down to the end of her nose. "I…can't."

"You can."

Janet closed her eyes, breathed in, and opened them. Picking up the bird and the marten, she left the theater behind, walking down the road as more snow started to cascade in on strong gusts. A park opened up on her left and she left the road to sit amongst the trees and the limestone statues and gaze at the pretty berries on the bushes. Leaving her fathers behind on the bench, she collected some and returned to them.

"I wish it were that simple," Hugh said. "We're already dead. Poison won't do it a second time."

Janet had almost forgotten. The only way they could die was with blunt force, something that would obliterate the brain…

She caressed the wrench on her belt and shook her head. "I can't do that."

"You must," he said. "If I could fly, I'd do it myself."

Janet gritted her teeth together until her jaw hurt. She

pulled the weapon from its holster and stared at the ground as tremors overtook her.

"Before you do this," Amos spoke solemnly, "I need you to know how much I love you. How much I regret not being there for you. I may not remember all of our time together but I will always remember you."

Janet nodded, fresh tears rippling down her cheeks as she uttered, "Love you, too."

"I'm proud of you, Janet," Hugh said, his eyes closing. "And I believe in you."

Lips trembling, Janet knelt to the ground in front of them. The air felt colder then, biting at her cheeks and her fingers. "I love you," she returned and swung her wrench high.

TWENTY

Janet only made it a few blocks before exhaustion folded down on her like night upon the day. She stumbled into the overhang of a building's entrance and buckled, lost in sobs and memories and everything that she'd been running from for years. Everything that had made her soft. Everything that had threatened her safety or her independence or her desire to make things right. Everything that she thought would magically be solved by the death of Steele, by the idea that she'd finally found her retribution.

It wasn't alright. Nothing was alright. They were still gone. The peace that she had thought she'd found after losing Amos the first time… Where was that when she needed it now? Why couldn't she take that and grab it by the gills and finally feel free?

Because, unlike all of the spells her parents had taught her as a child, overcoming loss wasn't magic. And she was sure that she would never be able to do it. Their deaths would always hurt.

Janet blew out a hot, rippling breath and gave herself a small slap on the cheek with her good hand. "Get up," she told herself. "This isn't the first time you've had to do this."

As she continued to walk the streets of Nothingland, she forced the thoughts of Amos and Hugh into the background and tried to remember as she'd done the morning after she'd left Town, the morning after her failure to kill The Man. She focused on her steps. She focused on the steady heel to toe motion of her feet and the sight of vapor as it pulsed from her frosty breaths. She listened to her heartbeat, to the steady whoosh of the air and how it darted around the buildings.

And soon enough, she stood outside of the Pancake House, its bright neon sign inviting her in. For a moment, the warmth and the light inside felt too good for her. She had never been a creature of comfort since losing her parents, why start now?

Because you deserve it, she imagined Hugh saying as if he was still with her.

She yawned open the door and stepped in. The hustle and bustle dwindled slightly at the sight of her. Janet glanced down at her torn and dirty clothing, her bruised hand, tousled hair and bloodied boots before shrugging and finding a seat at the counter.

Within moments, a waitress appeared, plopping a menu down in front of her and pouring a cup of coffee for her. As Janet went to curl her fingers around it, the waitress settled her hand on hers. "Are you okay?"

Janet looked up at the stranger: a woman she'd never interacted with before and saw the concern reflected in her eyes. Hell, maybe good people did still exist. She nodded. "No. But thanks."

With a small smile, the waitress asked, "What can I get

you?"

"Strawberry pancakes."

The waitress went to the kitchen to put in the order.

Sighing, Janet took her first sip of coffee in nearly three years. It was so damn good.

"Hey."

She looked over. The Mark took a seat next to her, his eyes scanning her. "You look like you've had a night."

"Yeah. It's been an interesting one," was all she could make herself say. She didn't want to get into the details and it seemed like the Mark recognized that. He calmly reached over the counter to the coffee pot on the opposite side and poured himself his own mug then gently topped off Janet's before putting it back.

"If there's a way we can just keep that coming, that would be great," she joked, sipping her mug again. Somehow, the second sip was even better than the first.

"Depends." He shrugged. "Are you skipping town or do you plan on hanging around a while? I could use someone here who can get things done. All you can eat coffee and pancakes on the house for the work." The Mark held up his hands. "When you're ready of course."

Work. Janet scanned the Mark, his punchable face, his Pancake House standing like a testament to normalcy and warmth against a bitterly dark world.

What was left out there for her? The train. Sleepless nights in cold derelict buildings. Huddling over smoke from a fire that wouldn't start because the sticks were too wet to burn. Stealing for food. Stealing for scraps of food. Time alone with her thoughts.

She didn't want that anymore. She wanted to be useful. She wanted to wake up with a purpose goading her on. She wanted to feel like if she was doing something for someone else at least she was doing something for herself. And maybe then the pain wouldn't slice her whenever she moved. Maybe it would only catch her now and again like getting a finger caught in the door. Maybe she would feel like being Ella again.

Someday.

Janet nodded. "Sounds like a plan."

The Mark offered her a hand to shake and she took it, even as his face slid into shock at the sight of it. "Is that... broken?"

She raised an eyebrow. "Probably."

"I'll call my friend. He's a doctor." After a moment, he squinted at her. "Somehow, I have a feeling we'll be needing his services a lot with you."

She shrugged. "Maybe."

In what felt like no time at all, the waitress returned with a stack of three golden pancakes, their tops glazed in butter and the sheen of strawberry syrup with little dollops of whipped cream spotted in two places for eyes while a long of a smile rounding out the bottom. Glimmering slices of strawberry were practically heaped on.

Janet abandoned all of her uncertainty about the future and threw herself into a collision course with a pancake-induced food coma.

That night, under the covers in the cot down in Hugh's secret room beneath the Pancake House, Janet dreamed of her childhood home. There were no shadows in her dream. There was no darkness. There was no sound at all. There was only a strange blotted sun, the kind she remembered in summer, mid-day that seemed to saturate everything beneath it. And there was Hugh, planting his herbs in their greenhouse, and Amos, washing dishes in the kitchen, whistling a soundless tune, and there was her.

She stood at the back door glancing back and forth between each of them and then to the fields behind their house. From the grass, a pair of foxes sprung up, laughing and chasing one another around. The bubble of mirth shot through her as she watched them scurry and play, watched as they wiggled their tails and pounced at each other, as they roughhoused and occasionally nuzzled.

When she turned to tell her father, she noticed Amos was gone as was Hugh from the greenhouse.

It was just her and the foxes.

Or maybe the foxes were them now. Maybe they had been reunited after all, the universe giving them a second chance to fall in love again, to laugh, to be carefree.

After all, foxes were magic, as her father had once told her. Maybe it wasn't a dream but a prediction of things to come. Maybe this was her parents' way of letting her know they were alright. That they would be alright.

And so would she.

Hugh will return
in 2025.

Janet will return
after she licks her wounds.

ACKNOWLEDGEMENTS

I'd love to tell you that this book wouldn't have happened without fans of Undead Folk. That book exceeded all expectation that I had from it. For me, it was an experimental attempt at minimalism, at grief horror in a fairytale/dystopian setting. But the truth of the matter is that I always intend to write one book before falling in love with the characters and the world and the setting. And soon enough, I'm planning a second one a month after the first book comes out.

And after I've written the second one, I'm realizing I need a third to finish the story.

Why didn't I just write a novel?

Because these books were meant to be exercises in minimalism. Because I didn't plan that far ahead. Because I like writing in short form and as it turns out, this series read so much better spaced out, with each book coming out in the season that it was written for.

I took risks. I don't know what I'm doing half the time when I leap into these worlds and you know what? That's exciting to me. I don't ever want to lose that feeling.

So, for those of you who have taken the journey with

Janet, and Hugh, I thank you.

And yes, while the main series of The Deadlands is complete, it does not mean that we won't see them again, because what can I tell you? I love writing them so much.

Thanks to so many unbelievably wonderful people in the horror community at large for reading and reviewing and believing in the series and in supporting me, and in recommending the book.

And thanks to my close friends and loved ones for enduring my year-long obsession with Janet and the undead foxes.

But it's not over yet.

photo © Colin Borowske 2021

Katherine Silva is an ace Maine horror author, a connoisseur of coffee, and victim of cat shenanigans. Her favorite flavors of the genre mix grief and existentialism which she combines with her love of the New England wilderness in her works. She is a three-time Maine Literary Award finalist for speculative fiction and a member of the HWA and NEHWA. Katherine is also editor-in-chief of Strange Wilds Press. You can find out all about her work at katherinesilvaauthor.com.

www.ingramcontent.com/pod-product-compliance
Lightning Source LLC
Chambersburg PA
CBHW020044310726
48970CB00007B/2400